I0658878

WALL OF DUST

a novel by

Timothy Niedermann

Deux Voiliers Publishing
Aylmer, Quebec

Wall of Dust is a work of fiction. Names, characters, businesses, organizations, places, events, and incidents are either the product of the author's imagination or are used fictitiously. Any resemblance to actual persons, living or dead, events, or locales is entirely coincidental.

First Edition

Copyright © 2015 by Timothy P. Niedermann

All rights reserved.

Published in Canada by Deux Voiliers Publishing

www.deuxvoilierspublishing.com

Library and Archives Canada Cataloguing in Publication

Niedermann, Timothy, 1953-, author

    Wall of dust / by Timothy Niedermann.

ISBN 978-1-928049-26-5 (paperback)

    I.   Title.

PS8627.I416W34 2015   C813'.6   C2015-903365-9

Cover Art - Igor Boudnikov

Cover Design - Ian Thomas Shaw

Legal deposit – Bibliothèque et Archives nationales du Québec, 2015

For Charlotte, Louisa, and Nathanael

Chapter 1

The hillside next to the school was covered with olive trees. They were old, most of them, but they were green again, with new buds beginning to show at the ends of the gnarled branches, the recurring miracle of life extracted from the dry, rocky soil. These trees distilled the harsh elements into the staple of local existence, and seemed immutable, rooted not just in this ancient ground, but in the patterns of all the human lives that had ever occupied it. Otherwise, the land was spare, the few scattered patches of grass and late spring flowers only confirming that here, in the relentless cycle of subsistence, it was the land, the earth itself, that gave life, was life.

Aisha passed this hill on foot every day on her way to class. Every tree, she knew, took more than a decade to bear its first fruit, but in return for those years of human patience came a tenacious, centuries-long stream of sustenance.

The men who attended the trees seemed as enduring and ageless as the trees themselves. Aisha knew them all, fixtures in the landscape of her village since she could remember. They were a never-ending certainty, engaged in an activity that was constant, rising or falling in intensity only with the seasons, ever circular, and in that, reassuring to her as she walked, always briskly, on the path that meandered between field, orchard, and dwelling, to arrive at the white cube that was the village's elementary school.

And what did they see when they saw her this day, these men who were fixtures among the trees? A young woman, dressed in a long, flowing dress that snapped with the energy of each step she took. The girl was pretty but clearly took no pains to look like anything other than what she was, a schoolteacher. She was young, very young it seemed to them, not mature in the way the olive trees were, but on the cusp of something else, a potential just about to bloom. She moved smartly, purposefully past them as if on another plane of being, connected to their own but somehow freer, full of the brightness, the liveliness that hope in the future brings.

She turned a bend in the path, around the shoulder of the hill behind which the school stood and she was lost from their view. As she left behind the last trees in the olive grove, she could now see the schoolyard, with its immense cedar in the middle providing a focal center to the play area as well as a spreading, tent-like shade from the heat of the sun. The gate was open, and children, some with beaten-up backpacks, others carrying plain cloth sacks bulging tightly with the outlines of books, were moving noisily toward the building's entrance, chattering, jostling each other, straightening up when they saw a teacher, and generally as bright and happy-go-lucky as children will be before the formality of the school day takes them in. Aisha stopped and smiled at the sight. It was mid-May, and the school year was almost over. A little more than a month left. They had come so far. She took her hijab out of her pocket and covered her head, as much to make herself seem older as to convey proper deference to tradition. A couple of the senior women teachers monitoring the gate shook their heads, gently disapproving of the free-spiritedness Aisha flaunted, but half envying it as well. Aisha then took her place in the herd, catching glances from those who were her students, and was charged by the prospect of a new day of getting active, inquisitive, and irregularly attentive young minds to accept into their heads those essential bits of learning they needed to carry them forward in life.

* * *

In Aisha's classroom in the village of Qalunya, just outside Ramallah, little hands fitfully grasped their pens, and faces looked with a seriousness that could not veil their apprehension, at the characters she had drawn on the blackboard to be copied. The hour was passing slowly. These were first graders, big kids now in their minds, learning serious things. Pairs of eyes went up and down, and up and down again, the children tracing the curves of each stroke in their minds before trying to set them down in ink exactly, properly, within the lines on the paper before them. Their earnestness was moving, Aisha thought, as she walked among them, correcting how one held his pen or how another shaped her letters.

"Sit up straight, Ahmad." This to a little boy hunched over his desk.

"Not so tight, Nassim. That's right." She smiled, sensitive to the thinness of the shell of confidence each tried to maintain for her benefit. She was young herself, of course, and had only been teaching a couple of years, but she knew that, to them, she was a pillar of age and authority, to be respected and even feared. Firm discipline was a given, even in the early grades, an attempt to create an island of structured security while so much outside of school was the opposite, a wilderness of uncertainty and fear. She felt herself, quite consciously, to be a shepherdess whose job was to nurture and protect her flock.

She loved teaching children to write. It was more than just giving them another mundane tool for future life, like so much of education was, however crucial the tool might be. The Arabic alphabet is unlike the rigid letters of the West, whose modern form was set by the stark lines and serifs of the Roman Empire's Latin, meant to be chiseled into cold stone. Arabic flows alive from the pen, a free expression of art and poetry that must not just be learned but must be tamed to be mastered. But it must be tamed with love and caresses, for it will rebel against force and frustrate any student not respectful of its spirit.

With each stroke, the letters of Arabic reveal on silent paper the sinuous music of the language—not just the language of today, but of all Arab history, evoking with its twists and curves the joy, suffering, achievements, failures, but, most of all, survival of a people. Sometimes Aisha's eyes rose from the heads of the children industriously at work to glance out at the damaged buildings and mounds of debris that surrounded the school. The scars on her town were nothing to the scars on her soul though, for she shared in the collective sadness that only a people whose glory is in the distant past can feel. Yet she was not one to look back. She chose to look beyond—beyond the past, beyond the present, beyond rich and poor, beyond anything that shackled children and their dreams. She returned her gaze to her students and smiled, for this was the future glory, she felt. These little heads on these little bodies would leave the past and present behind to build something better. And she was their guide and protector to see them through.

At noon they went out to the courtyard to eat their lunches under the wide shade of the cedar. The children sat primly on the benches with their paper bags on their knees. Many ate slowly, making each mouthful last. The boys finished first and began to play games—chasing each other, stirring, stoking, revelling in the joyous noise of wild abandon. The girls took longer to eat and took the time to pack up the remains of their lunches and put them away. Then some joined the boys' frolic, while others played quietly under the tree until Aisha clapped her hands to call them together and head back inside.

The first lesson of the afternoon was nearly over when a dull pop interrupted the near silence of the scratching pens in the classroom. Aisha started. She knew what it was, everyone did, for it was a familiar sound. A homemade mortar was being fired over the wall into Israel. Every so often, a few militants—who knew who anymore?—would climb to just below the crown of one of the hills that looked down on the wall that separated the Palestinian West Bank from Israel. They would send a few shells across, sometimes aiming at a military outpost, sometimes at houses, often at nothing in particular, just toward whatever happened to be within range. This time, though, the sound was very loud; their position was close to the school. Aisha strode quickly, but not hurriedly, to the window, so as not to frighten the children with the near panic she felt in her gut. Not a hundred meters away, in a group of trees near the top of the hill, three men hunched over what looked like a short, thick pipe. She watched them drop a shell into it and saw the mortar bounce as it sent the projectile into the air. She heard the impact a few seconds later, a small muted thud, revealing nothing about where it had landed or what it had hit.

The pop of the mortar continued irregularly for several minutes until the whole classroom was motionless, staring at the teacher, eyes widened with concern. There was a collective holding of breath, waiting for the sounds to stop before the tension could be released and the next breath taken. But this did not happen.

Instead, they heard something else: a deep beating, far away but getting nearer and louder very fast. The children, already still, froze. This sound, too, they knew, and it always came from the south, always from the direction of Jerusalem. It was the gunships. They crossed the skies often—fast, black, primeval shapes bent with armament, angled forward as if intently searching the ground below. The beat of their rotors extinguished all other sounds, pushing not just your ears but your whole body to the limit of tolerance, the horrifying, omnipotent weight of sound bearing down upon you with an invisible force so intense it acquired a thick, smothering substance. So much sound that it was no longer sound, only a merciless pressure, bending you to the ground, your eyes and ears closed in pain for a few long moments before the pain receded and the weight slowly lifted and vanished, leaving for a few moments an empty quiet in its wake.

They heard the ominous approach, but the gunship did not pass overhead. The expected crescendo of the rotors never got close. Instead, suddenly and in quick succession, explosions hit the hill. Concussive blasts shook the school, and dirt showered the windows. A child screamed—they all screamed. Nothing could be heard but explosions and screaming. Then the wall of the classroom disintegrated, the roof collapsed, and Aisha, struck on the head, lost consciousness.

* * *

Aisha opened her eyes. She was outside, lying on the ground. There was a bunched-up cloth under her head—her hijab. Feet moved by her face; voices shouted. She propped herself up on one elbow and turned toward the school, her classroom. All she saw was broken rubble with people standing in it digging, throwing chunks of cinder block to the side. She tried to sit up, but dizziness overcame her, and she had to lie back down. She must have passed out again, for the next thing she was aware of was wailing, unrestrained eruptions of grief coming from her left. She leaned over on one arm, turning her body toward the sound. A number of bodies, mostly small, lay on the dirt in a row, jackets and sweaters improvised as sheets to shield their dead faces. A number of women in headscarves bent over the shapes, crying loudly and thrashing to and fro as if trying to shake off the distorted irreality of a nightmare. But the horror merely twisted around them more tightly, irreversibly, in response to their struggles. Two men deposited another small

8

form beside the others and returned to the destroyed school.

"Aisha, are you all right?"

It was Fajer, the Grade 4 teacher. She knelt beside Aisha and looked her over.

"They've called for help. We'll get you to the hospital."

Everything was disjointed. Aisha could see only what was in front of her, and the colors were too strong and hurt her eyes. Sounds came in snatches—the school principal, Abu Rafiq, yelling into a cell phone, a child crying, someone moaning, a woman screaming, a distant siren getting closer, a dog barking, a car horn being pressed over and over.

"No. I'm fine. Just give me a minute. I'll help."

There was a tingling in the pocket of her skirt—her cell phone. With a clumsy, disconnected hand, Aisha fished it out and pressed the button to answer the call.

"Aisha!"

"Mother. I'm fine. I'm fine."

"What happened? The school . . . "

Aisha let her mother go on in an unpunctuated stream of questions, the panic rising in her voice as if she had restrained it out of fear for her daughter and now could set it free. There was finally a pause.

"I'll tell you later. I'll tell you later. I've got to go. I need to help here. Don't worry. I'm all right, really. Bye."

She put the phone back in her pocket and sat still.

Fajer patted her on the shoulder.

"When you're ready. Take it slow." She rose and walked

9

off.

Aisha sat still for a few minutes, staring at the school building. The classroom where she had been teaching—moments ago, it seemed—had only its internal walls standing. The flat-roofed, one-storey building had collapsed, and her former classroom was filled with the remnants of the ceiling and roof. How she had survived, she did not know.

On the other side of the schoolyard several groups of children sat under the cedar tree, huddled together, scared but alive. Aisha thought she recognized one of the groups—her class. She stood up slowly and waited for some lightheadedness to pass, then began to walk haltingly toward them. One child saw her and raised his head slightly, but his gaze was flaccid and empty. An improvised bandage of someone's shirt obscured most of his head, and blood was caked on the side of his face. She had to limp closer to tell who it was. It was Karim. Her eyes went to the others. All but one were bandaged on the head. One boy had his arm in a sling. It was Hassan. A girl's face, looking up at Aisha, was lined with browning scratches of dried blood—Nada. Not one of their faces had any expression. They looked at her blankly, looked past her without speaking. Karim, Hassan, Rabia, Leila, and Nada. Five. There had been seventeen in the classroom today when she'd begun. She turned her head and looked again at the row of bodies. It was longer now and stretched to the wall. There were two rows. In the second row there was movement—heads being

10

propped up, bandages applied, reassurances uttered. Those children were alive. An ambulance had arrived; another could be heard approaching, its sirens wailing. Something in its sound resonated mournfully as if it knew it was coming too late for some.

More adults—parents, relatives—were running through the gate, howling, weeping, frantic, their heads twisting back and forth, not looking at the bodies on the ground, trying to find a face among the living. Several, shoulders hunched, wiping tears from their faces, began to walk along the rows of bodies, living and dead, looking at them slowly, one at a time, in no hurry to find proof of their worst fears. Aisha watched numbly as, one by one, they found their children, kneeling to touch the wounded hesitantly, afraid to break them further, or collapsing beside a still form, wailing anew, arms raised up, appealing to someone, something, to change what had happened, to retrieve the life that had flown away, to explain why. The wailing continued until the voices grew hoarse, audible scars on the flesh of the air itself. There came, of course, no answer, no explanation. Only the addition of other voices to the sorrow as each family found its own, each new voice deepening the pool of grief filling the schoolyard.

Aisha sat on the ground next to the remnants of her class. Hassan reached over to her, and she put her arms around him. The others moved nearer, and Aisha became the center of a human ball, the children grasping her waist, she with her arms around all of them as best she could, pulling them tighter and tighter. Braced by her familiar body, a couple of them began to cry softly, burying their faces in her clothes, hiding their eyes from all that was going on around them. They sat for a long time until, one by one, their parents found them. Catching sight of a small, familiar head and body clinging to Aisha, the parents' faces, ashen and hollow with anticipation of the worst, would explode into pinkness and tears at finding their child alive, and they ran over, convulsing with relief and gratitude, dropping onto their knees as Aisha relaxed her grasp enough so the child could be taken up into outstretched arms. The children, relieved and exhausted, dug their fingers into the sanctuary of their parents' clothing. And the parents, with eyes now only for the living soul they held tightly, desperately, carried their children slowly out of the schoolyard and did not look back.

Finally, Aisha was alone, still sitting on the ground, her back to the scrapes and grunts of the continuing rescue and triage in the schoolyard, to the voices of pain and loss. It took a while for her to find the will to move. Then she sighed and stood up. Only at that moment did she turn around. She limped, a sharp pain in her hip, to where the other parents stood. Most were now silent, depleted, finding from somewhere enough emotional stamina to watch over the little, imperfectly shrouded figure at their feet until it was taken away. Aisha said nothing, but embraced each man and woman there, briefly though, unwilling to intrude upon the private, unsharable grief of a parent who has lost a child. She went to lean against a fragment of the wall of the school that was still standing. Supported by the last bricks of what had been her present and future, lethargy overcame her. She closed her eyes and felt her body heave as swells of loss and grief hit her and hit her again, battering her insides until she couldn't feel anymore. Time stopped; the pain became a constant. She waited for the catharsis of tears and the release they would bring, but they didn't come.

Unable to move, unable to speak, Aisha watched the succession of rescuers, searchers, and mourners. Time meant nothing, just changes in heat and light. Its substance had vanished. Each moment on this spring afternoon was an empty eternity. A light breeze rustled the branches in the cedar—other rhythms, other forces, moving as they always had, but somewhere else now.

The last of the injured was finally loaded into an ambulance and driven away. One ambulance remained, parked outside the schoolyard. Its rear door was opened, and one by one, the little bodies were lifted, carried to it and softly, carefully slid inside. It seemed to take a long time, until the last was laid alongside his schoolmates and the door closed. The ambulance drove away with no lights flashing. There was no more urgency. The few people who were still there moved out of the yard and down the road until they were out of view.

Aisha leaned against the broken wall staring at the

empty schoolyard. It was now late afternoon, and the wind was rising, as it always did at this time of day, when the schoolyard was as empty as it was now. The wind began to kick up dust devils, and the angled light filtering through the branches of the olive trees backlit their edges, turning them into sprites rising out of the soil. She watched as they tore around the playground heedless of anything but celebrating their momentary existence, bouncing and swirling excitedly but so briefly, dissipating with the next gust, but quickly replaced by another and then another. The wind went on breathing life into dust for some time, and as long as it blew, the playground was restored, with at least a faint, straining echo of the aimless joy it was meant for. But eventually the breeze died down, shadows brought sobriety to the spaces that minutes earlier had been radiant, and Aisha realized it was late. The schoolyard was now truly empty. Out of habit, her feet moved toward the path home. Her mind followed her body obediently. But as she passed through the gate of the schoolyard, she felt a tug, a snag on her hem, then a slow, almost regretful release. Aisha lifted her skirt to keep it from getting caught again. She walked slowly back through the ancient olive trees, in and out of their long shadows.

* * *

As the school building was unusable and would have to be rebuilt, the decision was made to erect tents on the

14

playground to serve as temporary classrooms. The weather was warm, and this was an inexpensive solution. The teachers took the next few days to salvage what materials they could—locating books in the debris, seeing which tables and chairs could be salvaged or repaired, and which would have to be thrown out. Volunteers from the village set up several tent frames and stretched cloth over them. The cloth was thin, but it would do as shelter against the sun. Not against the rain, though, but there was no need to worry about rain at this time of year. They were able to squeeze six tents into the schoolyard—one for each class—and still have some space left for the children's recess.

School began again the next Monday. Funerals had been held on the weekend for Aisha's students. Theirs had been the only deaths. A teacher and two students from Grade 3 were still in the hospital with injuries, but all were expected to recover fully. The teachers came early and lined up together near the entrance to the schoolyard to welcome the children back. Several teachers wore black in mourning. The children began arriving soon after, many also wearing black. They were quieter than usual; no jostling or joking or chasing each other around the schoolyard. They looked at the tents, curious about their new classrooms, and seemed awed by the ruined school building. The teachers took charge, guiding the children to their proper tents and getting them busy as soon as they sat down, to push the transition back to something close to normal. It was an effort of resilience and determination, something new yet familiar, something that could help them leave the trauma behind as soon as possible.

Aisha threw herself into it. Her injuries still bothered her, but the pain had subsided to the dull throb of a nagging reminder. Swelling and some ugly bruises remained as well, but these were under her clothes, and though the pain would spike back if she moved the wrong way, they were not visible to others. She stood with the rest of the teachers and greeted her students, one by one, as they came through the gate. They formed a little ring around her, standing close, and she felt several fingers take hold of the fabric of her skirt. When they had all arrived, she guided them to their tent. She had arranged five desks in a row in front of the folding table that was serving as her desk. On the portable blackboard she had written a short, simple children's poem, and she set them to work copying it. The children bent over their papers and their pens began to scratch the words, letter by letter, syllable by syllable. Each face was taut with concentration. Rabia asked to begin again when the stroke of one of her letters accidentally touched another. Hassan and Leila immediately pleaded, "Me, too. Me, too." Their efforts pained Aisha. They weren't as confident, as fluid as they had been. Karim complained that his fingers hurt.

"Try not to hold your pen so tight."

"But I have to. I'll lose it if I don't."

Nada, normally bold and exact, was writing so small it was nearly illegible. They all seemed so intent, dutiful, clearly wanting to please. But it was joyless for them, and Aisha saw that. She helped them as best she could, but when they were done, they looked exhausted. Aisha had wanted to start where they left off, to give the children a sense of continuity, stability, as if nothing had happened. But something had happened, and there was no continuity. Their world had crumbled around them, and whatever sense of safety and hope they may have had lay smothered under the ruins of the school around them.

She looked around at the other tents. All were full, and there was a low murmur of activity coming from each. Teachers were pointing at blackboards, the fourth graders were all reading, and Sadid, their teacher, was walking quietly among them. A hand shot up in the Grade 6 tent. She couldn't tell what subject it was—probably math. The students tended to ask the most questions in math. Despite the tents, despite the ruined building behind them and the horrible memories of last week that she was sure the children in every grade held, a normality was struggling to assert itself, to reassure them it was still there.

She returned her attention to her own tent. The space behind the thin row of five makeshift desks was empty, only bare dirt. There were no other little desks reserving a spot for a tardy or absent child. There was no one else coming. She could still see and hear, in her mind, the faces of the children who should have been there, the sounds they made— animated, happy, trusting. Those faces and voices were gone.

Death had left only images and echoes within her, recollections that, she knew, would gradually grow dim. The empty floor stretched before her like the earth on their graves. She had lost them once to a rocket and would lose them again to time. She closed her eyes.

"Teacher?"

Aisha opened her eyes and saw five expectant faces in front of her, asking silently, "What do you want us to do next?" She felt empty, leaden. She moved back to her chair. There was a small stack of books on the right side of her desk. She chose one and looked up at the children.

"Who would like me to read a story?"

The children smiled and raised their hands to say yes. Aisha brought her chair around to the front of her desk and sat down. Settling the book in her lap, she opened it and, after a short pause when she couldn't seem to find her place, she found a familiar title, one she had loved from her own childhood, and began to read.

Chapter 2

The week ended. Aisha sat with her parents at dinner on Friday evening. Her mother served in silence and they began to eat. After a few mouthfuls, her father, Khalid, put down his fork and looked at her.

"How is everyone at the school holding together?"

Aisha didn't answer. She closed her eyes and her face tightened. They expected her to weep, for tears to release part of the pain they knew she must feel. But she didn't cry. She sat still and silent. No sobs escaped her; no tears leaked from her eyes. She was rigid, her head down, her face pallid and drawn, an invisible tension pulling at every corner of it. Her parents looked on, unsure of what to say or do. No one ate. Then, abruptly, Aisha stood and left the table. She returned to her room and closed the door softly, silently, until her parents heard the slight compression of wood on wood as the door eased finally into its frame and shut her in.

Aisha lay on her bed in the dark with her eyes closed and felt waves of emptiness pass over her. It was worse than pain. It was desolation. Shutting her eyes did nothing to shield her from the sensation that she was floating in space, staring into a dark unbroken infinity. The exertions of the past few days had channeled her grief, she had thought. Everyone at school was trying to get past what had happened, move forward together. But today the eyes of the living students looked like wells of sadness. She had felt powerless. It had taken all of her concentration and energy to stand in front of what was left of her class and pretend that they could go on as before. She had no strength to take their hands and guide them through the valley of doubt and fear that they had now entered. She had nothing to give them, nothing. Images overran the passage of time. Faces and forms flashed by, familiar yet just beyond recall. Lurid colors shouted soundlessly and concussed against the backs of her eyes in the dark. She lay motionless beneath their onslaught, breathing in desperate gasps as her torso was crushed down, down against the earth. Exhaustion finally smothered her torment. She drifted into semi-consciousness, then into a fitful, superficial sleep that gave her no rest.

* * *

Aisha did not leave her room the next day, or the day after that. She didn't go to school on Monday. Late that afternoon, Hana, her mother, knocked softly on the door. There was no answer, though she knew Aisha was awake. She knocked again, and there was still no answer. She turned the handle and gently opened the door. Muted light from the curtained window revealed a chair, a desk, and a bed where Aisha sat with her back to the window, her hair draping her shoulders in stringy locks, her eyes half open, staring down at nothing on the floor.

"Aisha?" No response.

Hana stood in the doorway, looking down at her daughter.

"Aisha?"

Aisha's eyes moved slowly toward her mother and then back to the place on the floor. Hana did not move, just watched. After a few moments, with a deep sigh that seemed to expel the lifeless air that had held her, Aisha straightened her back and raised her eyes.

"Aisha, there is someone to see you. It's Abu Rafiq from the school. Can you please come out and speak to him?"

Aisha hesitated a moment, then stood stiffly, reluctantly. She quietly followed her mother into the main room of the house. Her mother joined her father next to a tall, simply dressed man with a pale face and sagging eyes. Abu Rafiq's thinness made him seem taller than he was, and in his middle-aged, grey-haired presence, Aisha always felt herself recede into a smaller, girlish frame.

"Hello, Abu Rafiq."

Even in the small room, the others could barely hear what she said.

Abu Rafiq looked at his youngest teacher. She had lost weight, and the curved cheek of the young woman he knew had been replaced by a straight line, a tautness.

"How have you been, Aisha?"

A moment passed. Her head was turned, her eyes fixed on the window.

"I don't know. Not well, I suppose."

She started to raise her hand as if to prove her point, but stopped and put it down at her side again. Her mother ushered her to a chair and signaled for Abu Rafiq to take a seat. He went over to the wooden chair that was offered, but remained standing.

"Do you think you are almost ready to come back to school? We miss you. And there is a lot to do. The school year will be over in a few weeks."

"I don't know. I don't know. I don't think I can. I can't."

"The children need you, Aisha. You're their teacher."

"What's the point? They're dead. They're all dead. Everyone died. Can't you see?"

"I don't understand, Aisha." Abu Rafiq leaned forward. "You say everyone died, but they didn't. Most of the children at school survived."

"Oh? They survived? They are the same children? They

still have hope? They still want to grow up to be doctors and teachers? Have you looked at them? Look again. They all died. Every one."

Abu Rafiq pulled the chair around so it faced her and sat down. Aisha's eyes were fixed on the hands in her lap. She was taking long breaths, deep breaths, in and out, one after the other, sucking the air in and expelling it with no pause. The room filled with their sound and their urgency. Abu Rafiq waited. Khalid patted his wife's arm.

The breaths quieted. Abu Rafiq straightened in his chair and leaned toward Aisha.

"What can I do for you?"

Her eyes rose, and she exhaled a sigh.

"I don't know. Nothing. I'll be all right, I think. My mother is worried. She says I don't eat and I should eat. But I don't feel hungry."

"You should listen to your mother."

Abu Rafiq stood.

"We need you back, Aisha. The children need you. They lost their classmates, and now they think they have lost you. They need their teacher."

Aisha was nodding.

"I know. I'll be there tomorrow. I promise."

"Thank you."

He went to the door.

"Take care of yourself. It's horrible and sad, but it's the will of God, and there are children who still need you."

She looked up at him but said nothing. He tried to read her face but couldn't. He turned to leave.

"They still need me."

"Yes, they do."

But when he reflected upon it later, he wasn't sure she had meant the same thing as he had.

* * *

Abu Rafiq walked back to the school, using the same path he knew Aisha took. The children needed her to come back, as he had said, but the truth was that he needed her, too. He could probably find one of the other, older teachers to fill in. They had done that for each other numerous times before— for illness, childbirth, funerals, family issues. That wasn't it. No, he needed her to come back because he was afraid he would lose her, just like so many before. He had known her since she was a student at this same, now ruined school. It wasn't so long ago.

The villages tried to hold on, but it was clear that, for the most part, only older people remained. The youth had left and raised their families elsewhere. Some in the cities, some —the lucky ones who could get Israeli permission—abroad. They didn't come home to stay, just to visit. Some never came back at all. Unlike so many of her classmates, Aisha had stayed. She hadn't liked living in the city during university, she said. And she wanted to be a teacher, so uncommon these days. Most young people wanted money and new horizons. The dusty old village held little for them except memories of play, and play wasn't serious. Play didn't buy you a car.

What was there to do here? Abu Rafiq stopped and looked back at the village from where he was, halfway up the side of the hill, almost to the olive grove. There it was, small and quiet. The only sounds were a few children's voices, laughing, shouting, carried up to him on the wind. The crunch of a single car's tires on the gravel road rose and fell. A bird twittered abruptly, urgently. A hawk's sharp cry came from above. The strong preying on the weak. Well, who said nature was kind? Nature was hard, and village life, if nothing else, was close to nature. Life here could be hard. And it was modest. You didn't grow rich in a village, not this one anyway. You did what your parents did. Worked in the fields and orchards, practiced a craft or a trade in a small way.

Abu Rafiq didn't really believe that, but change is hard. Leaving is easier. There were those living here who commuted to Ramallah. Not many, but the numbers were growing, slowly. And that meant that he hadn't had to close any of the grades, not yet. He hoped it was a trend. The drive didn't even take that long, as long as a checkpoint didn't appear out of nowhere—they did that often enough. But that was an excuse, not a reason. He lived in Samana, a bigger village. It had a couple of shops and more commuters, since it was that much nearer to the main road. But Samana wasn't Ramallah. And Ramallah wasn't America. There was always a bigger lure for the ambitious. No, that wasn't right, or at least he didn't look at it that way. It depended what your ambitions were, what your vision of your future was. But maybe he was naïve.

He wanted to create a wonderful little school. Full classrooms, satisfied teachers, happy children. Ambitious to be sure. And that was why he needed Aisha. He needed young teachers to grow with the school, who could keep up with all the change in the world. The older ones were being left behind, and you couldn't ask them to catch up. Here there was a gap, too. The young ones wanted to work abroad. There were few jobs here. Some taught for a while, but they jumped at the first lucrative-looking opportunity elsewhere. He could count five, no, seven of his teachers in the past few years who had left the country for good. He knew Aisha wouldn't leave, not for that reason. But he was worried about her. She had obviously taken the loss of her kids hard. Well, she wasn't alone. There was a dark weight in everyone's heart still. You grow older, you see things that life does, and you harden. She hadn't hardened—not yet. She expected life to be full for every one of her students, not snuffed out from the sky on a sunny day.

That it was an accident just made the whole thing so horribly mundane, capricious. The will of God. It was life, life here anyway. He hated to say it, but most of the people

26

he knew had seen such tragedies before; it wasn't new. They had lived through horrors of war and disease and suffering and death, and most had found a way to move forward. With sadness, a sadness that never really lifted, but they were used to it. That's why so many left; they didn't want to get used to it. He didn't blame them.

Would Aisha get used to it like he had, like people his age had? He hoped not, but he needed her to. She had to pull herself together for the children who were left. They were dazed still, in shock, in need of reassurance. She was too important to them. He hoped she realized this.

Now he was in the olive grove. He loved these old trees. They had been here when he was a boy. The trees were reliable in a way few things are. Tough, a product of this difficult land. They had always been there. He used to play in this orchard, running, hiding among the trees. He could almost name them. Funny, he had never tried. He wondered what names he would use? It was an odd thought. Should they be names of friends or elders? Should they be serious names, names with history and meaning, like those of the ancient prophets? But many people bore those names. So how could he name the trees right? Maybe you couldn't. Maybe that's why he never did.

He came to the rise just above the school and looked down. The debris of the shattered building had been cleaned up, but the destruction was obvious. A few walls and rooms still stood, but they weren't sound any more. Classes were being held in the large tents that filled most of the playground. They were lucky with that playground. It had always seemed like such a wonderful space, a free space to run, a safe place. That was an illusion, a fantasy of childhood, created by the low wall that surrounded the yard and by the shelter that the spreading branches of the cedar offered. Adults knew better how flimsy such things could be; it was the protection of an embrace, not of thick walls and a wide roof. He wanted that feeling of safety back, for the children and for himself. And he thought it was possible. The school was destroyed, but the tree and that low wall were untouched.

The whole structure would have to be torn down and rebuilt. He had already been in contact with the education ministry for funds. There wasn't much money available. He would have to raise some from the community. Luckily, there were plenty of men in construction around who could contribute their time. Many of them were out of work right now. So it was materials that were lacking. He would find a solution. The big question was whether to build here, in this spot, or somewhere else, maybe even in another village, one farther away from the wall. He was uncomfortable with that, but unsure why. Maybe it was just that he had gone to school here and didn't want to change. Or maybe he didn't want to give up. That felt better in his mind. Was it true? Or was he just set in his ways like his elders? A grandfather before his time.

Some said it would be better not to rebuild at all. They could consolidate their school with another, since so many had extra space. That meant arranging transportation, probably using buses, but it could be done. It didn't feel right, though. It felt like giving in. It felt like dying. In his mind, he was planning a new school for right here where it belonged. To reassure the community that it would endure.

It would take some persuasion. Many in the village were fatalists. It was all the will of God. That and a shrug were all they had to say. They would go back to their lives, gathering to them what pieces were left. It wasn't enough for him. He hoped he wasn't insensitive. He didn't think so. But if it was the will of God that the school was destroyed, it would be the will of God to rebuild it. Of this he was sure.

Chapter 3

"Your hijab!"

"Oh! Yes. Thank you, mother."

Aisha wrapped the cloth absently around her head as she left, not saying anything more. Hana watched her go, disconcerted. Aisha did not look well, and she had not eaten anything.

Aisha returned at the end of the day and went straight to her room. A little over an hour later, Hana knocked on her door and opened it.

"Aisha?"

The young woman looked up at her mother. Aisha's face was bloated and her eyes were red, with dark smears under them. Light glistened from the wetness on her cheek.

"Aisha, are you all right?"

Aisha said nothing, just looked at her mother as if she were speaking nonsense. Hana came to the edge of the bed and sat next to her. She put an arm around Aisha's shoulders and squeezed. Then she put her other arm around her daughter and hugged her as hard as she could.

"It's the will of God. There is nothing we can do."

Hana stroked Aisha's hair and kissed her on the head.

"It's the will of God to kill little children? Little babies?" Aisha's voice was strained, nearly sobbing. Her mother hugged her tighter.

"I know it's hard to understand. I don't understand it either. It's such a waste. Those poor little children."

"They deserved to live."

"Of course they did."

Mother and daughter sat in silence for a long time, arms around each other—the one desolate, inconsolable; the other not knowing what to do, other than to be there in the room. Finally, Hana stood up.

"I have to make dinner. Your father will be home soon." She moved toward the door, but at the threshold she turned.

"It's the will of God, my child. You must try to accept that."

"I can't. I just don't understand."

"The will of God is beyond our understanding. We can only have faith."

"But why? What did they do to deserve to die? Does faith give us a reason for that?"

Hana tensed. This was irrational.

"Our faith is the only thing that will get us through such things as this. It's all we have."

"I have no faith anymore."

"Don't say that." Hana walked back to Aisha and put her hand on her shoulder. "It wasn't your fault. You'll see. Right now it's hard, I know. You're hurt. You're upset. Something truly horrible has happened, and you need time to recover. But you will, don't worry. You'll see. You'll believe again— in God, in yourself." She leaned over and kissed Aisha one more time, then turned and left the room.

Aisha continued to sit, not moving, staring at the wall of her room but not seeing anything. A few minutes later, she stood and went to find her school bag. From it she took out the book she had been reading to her students. She read slowly, holding onto every word, reluctant to let any go. When she finished the story, she leaned back and closed her eyes. Images swirled—faces, colors, sweeps of cloth over forms moving across landscapes saturated in magic. She inhaled the scents of strange blooms, the smells of earth and sky, tightened her eyes against the vivid sharpness of each line, each smile, each leaf, and let herself sink into an unending moment of childhood again. She lived only in this instant—there was no *gone*, no *to become*, only *is*. One single, infinite moment. Her skin began to tingle with the redemption of it, and the sensation sank into her. It filled her, immersed her until it was her world. It was the awareness of dream-filled sleep. So clear, so alive. Then the cold impossibility of it all reached her, and the moment shattered. The colors faded; her numbness returned. Her mind rose again, and she blinked at the shadowed room.

"Aisha! Can you come help me in the kitchen?"

Her mother's voice, the sound more than the words, made her close the book. With the reflex of years of being her mother's helper, she walked to the little kitchen where her mother was cutting up a chicken.

"Could you chop these for me?"

An onion, a cauliflower, and an eggplant lay on the counter—*maqluba*. They had it every weekend, the only time they could count on eating together properly, as a family. A knife lay on a wooden cutting board that was beginning to warp with age. It had belonged to Hana's grandmother, one of the few things that generation had been able to pass down. One side had been used so much that the center of the surface was rounded inward. Aisha turned the board over to use the flatter side and scraped the blade of the knife with the pad of her thumb. The edge felt too dull. She found the sharpening stone in the cupboard and placed it on the counter. She angled the knife by resting it on her hand as her mother had taught her and began to grind the blade, sliding it away from her slowly. Ten times on the coarse side of the stone, ten times on the fine side. She tested the edge again and was satisfied.

Her mother looked over her shoulder at Aisha.

"You need any help?"

"No. I know what to do."

Hana turned back to separating the drumstick from the thigh.

The onion should be first. Hana would sauté it quickly in oil, then add the chicken. Aisha picked up the onion, turned it on its side, and placed the knife on its broadest part, its equator. Her hand was practiced, sure. How many times had she reduced an onion to a useful mound of almost identical squares, ready for the pan? The blade, with the slightest motion of her wrist, made a tiny slit in the onion's papery outer skin. The flesh was exposed. She couldn't bear it.

She put down the knife and with two hands put the onion aside. She picked up the knife again. With the other hand, she grabbed the cauliflower. She would begin with that, doing things in reverse. The surface looked like a canopy of little trees sprouting outward, but bound to the stalk. She would free them. With a familiar, confident precision, she began to cut. When the stalk was bare, she took the little trees and lined them up in rows, like a miniature orchard on the counter top, before pushing them into a pile and moving the pile to the side.

Aisha picked up the eggplant. Its purple skin shone. She breathed out. The eggplant was beautiful. But it could not be eaten like this. She raised the knife. She worked slowly, caressingly, with assurance, making each slice exactly the same thickness, as if they were all from the same mold, all of the same family. Then she set the slices down tightly together, overlapping so you could still see the shape of the eggplant but also see what was inside, what was to be cooked, eaten.

Her hand trembled, and she tightened her grip on the knife. She knew what would happen now with the onion. She could not caress it, love it, free it. She had to attack it, dominate it, control it. To be useful, it had to hacked into shards. A pile of debris. It would fight back, sting her, force her tears.

Aisha grabbed the onion like a ball, set it down on the cutting board, and, putting her whole weight behind the knife, cut the sphere in half, the blade hitting the old wood with a dull knock. She separated the two halves and used the tip of the blade to peel off the outer layers—the skin, the hide. Bending over, she placed the knife on the first whitish hemisphere and closed her eyes. She placed her palm on the top of the blade and felt it cut bluntly straight down, not a slice, using the sharpness of the blade, but a crush, using overwhelming, superior mass. She did this until the onion's flesh had collapsed into strips of broken rings. She took the second half and did the same. Now, there was nothing but shards in front of her. She began to mince, holding the blade with two hands—one on the handle, one pinching the tip—to keep her cuts even. Opening her eyes a crack as she chopped, Aisha saw pieces of onion fly off and drop onto the floor.

She bent to pick them up and then continued to dice. Her eyes brimmed over. Pieces slipped, avoiding the blade, and she had to change angles to make sure she cut each one.

The pieces grew smaller, more uniform. Over and over, eyes tight, she heaped the bits into a mound and leaned over to chop into and across what became a pile of little squares. All she heard was faint rips and the sound of metal on wood.

Aisha cut until her eyes stung despite being closed, and she had to turn away. At the sink, she washed her hands, her face, then bunched up a dishcloth and held it hard against her eyelids, so the pressure would smother the last traces of the pain. When she turned back, she saw no point in using the knife any further. The squares were small enough. She lifted the cutting board and dumped the onion bits into the bottom of the pot. Her mother came and poured a little olive oil over the onions before turning on the burners.

"Thank you. This will taste good."

Hana saw the exhaustion on her daughter's face.

"Are you all right?"

"I'm fine."

Aisha turned and walked into the next room. She found her book and spent several minutes sitting upright in her chair, her eyes closed again, the book held to her chest with both arms. She rocked back and forth as she filled her mind again with colors and smells, fleeting images that gradually slowed down enough for her to follow them. She was asleep when her mother looked in on her a little while later.

The next morning, Aisha walked her familiar route, tied her hijab on her head as she entered the school ground, and made her way to the tent where her class was already waiting. And she began to teach again. She stood in front of her five remaining pupils and tried to reignite the joy of learning within them. But she had no spark in her. She knew all they wanted was for her to be herself again, to help them forget, to give them back their little world where learning was not a job but a joy because of her. But she couldn't. She saw the bare ground behind their chairs that should have been obscured by other chairs and other faces. She found herself reading to them—stories about birds and ghouls, princes and poor boys—ancient fables and cautionary tales. They liked the stories. The wings of the words carried them to a place far away, a comforting place, a safe place. The children responded; each day they were more animated. They smiled more and joked with each other again and their eyes started to look eager again, not pleading. But the stories only saddened Aisha. Where the children heard adventures, she felt her mouth form words that hummed with the innocence of childhood, and she could barely stand it. She spoke the words almost without hearing them, barricading her mind against their pull. Every so often she would raise her eyes to look at the children, but found herself looking away, unable to cope with the raptness in their faces as they listened.

Aisha went back to teaching her class to write. She wrote simple sentences on a small chalkboard and had them copy the letters in silence. No poems. No cats, no dogs, only objects that were black or white, red or blue, big or small. Nothing alive. Nothing to open any doors inside her. She watched the children at recess. They ran around in the schoolyard, playing tag as if their very being required it. To Aisha, though, the small expanse of reddish earth seemed cavernous—cold and dark and empty in the sunlight. The laughter of the children seemed fragile. More laughter was needed to fill the space, to give confidence to the expression of youthful joy, but it was not going to come. Sobs tried to rise, but they merely gouged her insides, too deep within her to climb out.

On the last day of the week, Aisha again walked to school in a daze of exhaustion and numbness and again set the children to writing simple sentences about rocks and trucks, roads and buildings. But no names, no people. No trees, no flowers. The morning was windy, and dust blew through the tents, irritating the children's eyes, choking them and making it difficult for them to concentrate. Aisha's back was to it, and she hunched over to shield herself. Late in the morning, a few men came and tied bedsheets to the sides of the tents, blocking the wind. But the improvised walls flapped noisily and were almost as distracting as the wind and dust had been. Midday finally came. She picked at the lunch her mother had made for her, then put it down and forgot about it. She watched the children eat and play, but didn't really see them. Hassan skinned his knee and started to cry. Aisha didn't react until another teacher touched her shoulder and pointed him out. Lunch ended, and she tried to continue the day's lessons. The wind died down, and the tent grew hot. The children began to complain. Aisha managed to remove the sheet on her tent and let some air in. The children copied more sentences until the final recess of the day.

The children had been fidgeting for a while and bolted from the tent as soon as they were dismissed and went to play under the cedar tree, where it was cool.

For a long time, Aisha stood under the tent and looked out on the schoolyard toward the gate. The wind kicked up dust, and some grit got in her eye. She rubbed the eye as she continued to stare at the schoolyard. The wind moved across the empty part of the yard near the gate, kicking up little dust devils that jostled playfully, chasing and dodging each other for the brief instant they existed. The children saw them and raced after them, laughing. As each whirl of living dust spent itself and settled back to earth, it formed a little mound, and Aisha saw again the small, shrouded shapes lying still in the same dust, their playmates laughing and circling among them. The wind began to blow stronger, and the dust shapes rose with the wind once more, again and again, to join in the game. Aisha watched the ghosts rise and fall and their old playmates run among them, happy.

The wind died down and Aisha found herself walking

through the schoolyard toward the gate. The names came all at once into her head in an onrush that felt loud but was noiseless, a jumble of mute words beyond her mind's reach. Then they evaporated, leaving behind only a hint of what they were.

Her feet carried her out the gate and onto the path through the olive grove. She stumbled up the slope, her eyes fixed on the ground but not looking where she put her feet, which kept slipping on the loose stones strewn over the uneven ground. Her eyes found a sheep track. Her feet followed them onto it, and they let the track lead them around the hill. Aisha was conscious of little but the noise her feet made—the gritty sound of rough surfaces meeting, sand grating on stone. Her feet slipped time and again, and now and then she had to stretch out her hand to avoid falling. She fell several times anyway, and her hands bled from breaking her falls. But she didn't feel them, nor the impact when she fell the next time, and the next. She felt nothing—not the ground under her feet, not the sun, now hot, not the sweat that flowed under her shirt. Time did not pass. She did not look up.

She began to walk faster as she rounded the side of the hill. A voice muttered, "My babies, my lambs. My babies, my lambs." She heard it faintly in her mind from some place distant, but couldn't feel herself saying the words, though they grew louder, the faster she walked. And as the path rounded the hill and led down its slope, she began to run. As

40

she ran, the voice became a scream—"My babies, my lambs. My babies my lambs"—louder and louder. The sound of the screams filled her head as she ran downward, stumbling and tripping, barely keeping her balance.

Now she could hear the screams in her ears and feel them in her throat. She ran so fast that her lungs burned, but she pushed against the pain and screamed louder, gasping for breath. The unaccustomed exertion now was searing her legs. Her heart pounded against the sides of her head.

She stopped and bent over, out of breath, wincing with each heave of her chest. She couldn't breathe at all; her hijab was tightening around her throat. It was strangling her. She tore at the cloth around her neck, her head becoming light, her vision narrowing. Ripping and tearing, she finally freed herself from the black tentacle, then tossed the limp strip of cloth aside into the dust. She started off again, grabbing a stitch in her side at first, but then regaining her breath, her rhythm. Her lungs still hurt, but her legs, weary and heavy just moments ago, were numb; she could look down and see her shoes slap the earth but only perceive the impact as a distant observer. They moved mechanically by themselves. Her long hair now streamed over her shoulders and whipped in the air, unkempt and wild, stinging now and then when a lock whipped across her face. Her eyes were fixed on the ground, but what she saw was in her head: little bodies, hastily shrouded, lying under the cedar tree. She began to scream again, over and over, "My babies, my lambs. My babies, my lambs."

She rounded the hill, descending toward a valley floor. What rose into view was a road, an empty strip of land, and a stark, blank wall of mute concrete looming eight meters high, casting its long shadow on the ground in front of it and stretching as far as the eye could see in each direction. Every two hundred meters or so, a tall observation turret bulged over it. Each turret had a narrow window of darkened bulletproof glass at the top, allowing a 360-degree view of what was around and below—the eye of an automaton coldly taking in all that passed before it. The window was punctuated by gun slits giving clear lines of fire in all directions. The single, lightly travelled road ran parallel to the wall. There was nothing else visible. The Beitunya checkpoint was several kilometers to the east. It was just a slight interruption in the wall, really—a narrow, fortified gap through which Palestinians could pass, after a thorough search, to work for Israelis on the other side, though fewer and fewer were allowed to.

* * *

The soldiers in the observation post saw the woman come over the hill. She was running, and they could tell she was yelling something, but she was too far off, and it was unintelligible to them. Sergeant Zev Yadin, the sharpshooter on duty, chambered a round and glanced at his superior.

"Dani?" He used his superior officer's first name. This was habitual among the Israeli military, a relic of the glory days of the egalitarian kibbutzim, so long ago. He focused the crosshairs of his scope on the woman. She was now about 150 meters away.

"Wait."

At the bottom of the hill, the road was about fifty meters from the base of the wall.

"If she crosses the road and continues toward us, drop her."

The destruction of the school had only one consequence: the Israel Defence Forces were on high alert in this area for terrorist attempts at retaliation. Lieutenant Dani Elon stared through his binoculars to try to assess what was happening. Her clothes were loose enough to hide a dynamite belt, but he was doubtful. Still, protocol was firm: any apparent threat was to be eliminated well before the range within which any explosive device they might be carrying could inflict damage on the wall or observation post. And a dynamite belt could do a lot of damage; he had seen the aftermath of such attacks firsthand. The memory girded him.

Zev followed her with his scope. She was moving fast and erratically. A bad target. He liked them upright and still. He preferred a head shot; its success was unambiguous. But he would have to go for the body. She wasn't wearing the usual Arab tent. Her loose clothes were streaming behind her. He looked for any sign of a bomb. One big enough to do damage here would have to be bulky. He could see nothing. Then what the fuck was she doing?

As the woman neared the road, the two soldiers watched. But even as her form grew larger, it was still hard to gauge the sort of threat she posed. The woman came to the road and stopped. She was about a hundred meters or so up the road from the observation post. She stumbled over the drainage ditch on its far side, clambered up to the asphalt, then stopped. She stayed motionless for a while, then crossed the road, clambering down the embankment nearest the wall. She was running hard, her face distorted, screaming in Arabic, something that distance still prevented them from understanding. She was now fifty meters from the wall.

Dani saw that his choice was made.

"Take her out."

"I don't think she's wearing a bomb."

"I don't give a shit! Shoot her!"

Zev tensed, holding in his anger at Dani's tone. He squinted into his sight.

"What are you waiting for?"

Zev centered the image of the girl in his scope and took a breath. He held the air in for a moment, and as he let it out, in a slow, easy stream, his finger tightened around the trigger. The rifle spat. One hundred meters beyond Aisha a slight puff of dirt rose from the earth.

"Dammit Zev!" Dani lowered his binoculars and glared at the sniper. "How the hell could you miss that?"

Zev took his eye from the scope.

"Look. She stopped."

The binoculars rose to Dani's eyes again. The wind was billowing the woman's clothes, pulling them tightly to her, then swirling them around her form. It was clear she wore no explosives. She also looked young, more a girl than a woman.

"Okay. Belay that order. She's harmless. But what the fuck is she doing?"

Aisha stood stock still. She stared at the blank face of hardened concrete. The wall was constructed of giant slabs, standing shoulder to shoulder, rising out of the earth toward the sky. Their surfaces were smooth, uniform, faceless, blind, and their single row stretched to the limits of her perception on either side. She saw nothing but a gray vastness. Its dark shadow was nearly to her feet and made the ground open up into an enormous chasm; the wall was now a barrier of depth as well as height. She felt dizzy, on the edge of a bottomless precipice. The wall melted in front of her and she saw an olive grove with old trees. Branches of life. She steadied herself, but the gray returned and her vision swirled with it.

She could hear the wind blowing behind her but in front of her the air was still. She grew short of breath and stood back, inhaling deeply to recover. There was no motion at all —nothing—as if the world had stopped spinning and time had worn itself out. She took another step back, staring, trying to find a face in the void.

As Dani watched her, his eye caught something. Two, no, three people were rounding the hill with the olive grove, following the same course as the girl had. These also looked like women, he thought. He focused his binoculars. Two women and a man. They were running, but not fast, not nearly as fast as the first woman. They were waving their arms in the air and seemed to be yelling something as well.

"Zev, we have more company. Get ready."

Zev chambered another round. The group slowly approached the road.

"Steady."

Dani was looking as hard as he could at the faces.

"Steady."

The women and the man reached the road. The girl in front of the wall now saw them and began to walk toward them. Then she fell abruptly. She tried to get back up, but could only rise to her hands and knees. The others reached her and stopped. The women knelt to help her while the man pulled out a cell phone and made a call.

"Don't relax. Keep your sights on them."

"Yes, sir."

After maybe ten minutes, perhaps less, a small van came into view. It hurtled down the road and stopped in front of the group. The women helped the girl over to it and all got in. The van turned around and drove off in the direction from which it had come.

As the van disappeared around a bend in the road, Zev relaxed his grip on the rifle and took his eye away from the sight. It was now long past mid-afternoon and the shadows from the olive trees that dotted the hillside in front of him were beginning to creep down the slope.

Downstairs, Dani poured himself a cup of coffee and wrote a brief report, which he transmitted as soon as he was done. It said very little, but he was supposed to report everything.

Zev was now alone with the landscape that his weapon surveyed. It was a small landscape, the olive grove, the road to Ramallah. A few houses, but far off. Out of sure-kill range. He didn't like to take chances with his kills. None of them did, but he was very particular. They had to be clean. One shot, one body. No mess, no collateral damage, no unintended anything. No misses. Ever. Clean, they had to be clean.

His mother would have liked that. "Clean for the unclean," she would have said. He was sure of that. Even he wasn't clean enough for her. At least his dad wasn't. When she left it was because Dad was unclean. He heard her say it. Their house was small, his room next to theirs. He heard everything, pretty much. So did his brother, but he was younger and didn't get it.

She left with the rabbi and married him. He was clean. At her funeral the rabbi looked spotless. He hadn't wanted her first family there, but too damn bad. The three of them came, the filthy guys. The rabbi who had officiated at the funeral was someone else, someone from the settlement. "Vengeance!" he kept saying. "We must exact vengeance. We must take revenge for these murders against those who defile this land by their presence." The rocket attack had killed her as well as her baby. His sister. He had never met her. She was probably nice and clean. All babies are. They smell that way. Maybe he had too, but he guessed by the time he had his bar mitzvah he smelled different. Like a man. Like his dad.

The clean rabbi now had a bunch of children with some teenage virgin he married a couple of months after the funeral. They do that in the settlements; they get the girls busy pushing out babies. Nice, clean babies.

Zev was good with a rifle. They had noticed it right away in the army. He was nineteen and had never held a weapon before, but he had drilled each target in the center as if the rifle were a part of him. Easy with the M-14s they trained them on. A kid's weapon, he thought now. So he was assigned to a special unit where they gave him an upgraded . 300 M24 sniper rifle—a man's weapon with an effective kill range of twelve hundred meters. But you had to be closer to make sure of a clean kill. Close enough for the head shot.

"Clean," they all said, "Clean." It was drilled into every member of his team, shooters and spotters. Clean shot, clean kill, clean conscience. Your duty. These are bad men; they have killed Jews. They will kill more Jews if we don't kill them first. Be proud of what you do.

And he was the cleanest. Or had been. His last kill had been at over four hundred meters at night in Gaza. He had done his job; he had hit his target. Trouble was, it wasn't the right target. It was the man's brother—no one important. Intelligence had screwed up. So he had killed the wrong man, and the team had blown up the wrong room, or the right room with the wrong people in it. Women, a few children. They said five, but who knew? Only body parts were left. All collateral damage. The error had been hushed up; the real target was big and bad and most of the blame was put on him—as it should have been, for hiding behind noncombatants. Still, the unit had been quietly broken up, and he was here on temporary duty awaiting reassignment.

Zev watched the trees rustle in the wind. It had been hot here all day but was getting cooler, thank heaven. Was he upset, rattled? He didn't know. He honestly didn't know. He wasn't clean any more, in any case, one way or the other. So he hadn't shot the woman. He couldn't. He had sighted on a patch of ground a hundred meters beyond and had hit it squarely. He hadn't missed. He never did.

In a few hours it would be sundown, the beginning of Shabbat. This week, he had pulled Shabbat duty. Although military regulations gave extra dispensation for it, he'd never felt comfortable with the extra pay. To him, the week's work was never done. You could rest, reflect, worship, but you never lowered your guard. You couldn't. Ever.

Chapter 4

The doctor had told her to stay in bed, but on Sunday, lying awake, Aisha felt as if she were trussed on an altar in a tomb.

"Where are you going?" was all her mother got to ask before the front door closed behind her. The street was hot in the late morning. Aisha went right, then right again, then left, pivoting at each corner, zigzagging her way around her village. The streets were spare and clear, the houses plain— their outward sameness shielding the human variability within. The streets were not marked, but she knew them by heart. She twisted as she walked to touch the village air with her body, no thought in her head, just feeling the resonances of the stones, the masonry, the slow, warm breeze, and the spots of coolness in the shade. Sensation without reflection. She walked quickly in the heat but ignored her sweat. Her long hair spread wide on her shoulders, and she let it flounce and billow behind her.

When she reached the edge of the village, the road straightened before her, so she pivoted and took a goat track down into a ravine, across a small stream, then up the low rise on the other side. The rise gradually swelled into a long hill and when she reached its dome, she left the track to stumble through the scrub. The grass was still green in places, though it had started to dry, and the only shade came from the stunted olive trees in a couple of abandoned orchards.

Off the path, her progress slowed and her mind awoke. She picked her way among the grass and bushes, the rocks and infrequent trees, through the landscape in which she had lived her entire life—a familiar terrain grown foreign. She became aware after a while that she was talking to herself. The voice was as strange as her surroundings, and she listened to it as if it were a radio announcer or a voice-over on television. She didn't like what she heard, but let it go on, as there was nothing else. It was too sad, too sad, and made her heart hurt. Pointless, pointless. Smiles forever gone, sweet voices, not like this one. Gone, gone. She had to get back to the living, to the ones who still needed her, but all she could do was move her body, pump her limbs, give forward motion to a body that didn't know where to go.

The wind, which had confined itself to animating the grasses and trees, now enveloped her. It felt warm—not like the heat of the day, but like the warmth of a hand placed on her shoulder, an arm draping her sorrow—a silent presence that said without speaking that she wasn't alone. It felt kind. Aisha sat in the grass and let the wind flow over and around her. It was dry and weightless, carefree yet worn with time. She had known the wind on these hills since her childhood, a force of change and destruction, of cleansing and abundance. The wind carried both storms and rain, relief from the oppression of heat, and punishment for the naïve caprice of thinking nature benign. Now it made her a part of it and rose up to cup her face and shatter with its lightness the heavy gravity of her despair. She looked around her. Everything she saw was moving, alive. The grasses whipped, their ends snapping; tree limbs swayed and creaked. Earth rose as dust to dance among them while the rocks looked stolidly on, arbiters of nature's chaos. She might have been thrilled, she knew, but that was for later. Right now, she felt welcomed and consoled.

As Aisha sat, she both remembered and forgot. Time stopped and yet extended; she was wrapped in a moment and in forever. She felt comforted—comforted but not healed. This she understood. She lay down and let the earth, the grass, the soft air swaddle her. She felt warm. She basked in the sun, and she was a part of it all. She lay with eyes closed, seeing not darkness but yellow through her eyelids. She slept. And when a cooler breeze reminded her of who she was, Aisha stood up. She walked down the slope of the hill, the wind around her and at her back, until she reached the

Ramallah road. When she got home she was exhausted and collapsed into bed, to sleep through the night with no shadows of memories in her mind.

* * *

The weekend was quiet. It usually was, since Muslims observed their Sabbath on the same day as Jews. Few people travelled the road, although his vigilance was never relaxed —danger could come at any time and in so many forms: suicide bombers, car bombs, snipers, rockets, mortars. Zev was trained to catch the slightest hint of anything unusual— be it people moving oddly on the hillside or the slightest glimmer of purpose in someone's eyes—and to respond quickly and effectively, with maximum force, to neutralize the threat. It had been drilled into him: Israel's enemies needed only to win once; Israel had to win always, just in order to survive. And so it was, even in the thousands of daily interactions between Israelis and Palestinians. To drop one's guard meant that someone would die. To stand firm meant that the people whose lives might have been publicly shattered by a bomb lived another day in happy anonymity.

* * *

Shabbat passed, then Sunday. Zev had pulled checkpoint duty and spent the weekend at the Beitunya crossing. He hated it. It was always the same: quiet; a line of Palestinians waiting for hours in their cars, or standing or crouching by the side of the road, while the soldiers carefully, thoroughly searched persons, belongings, and vehicles. The hours passed, and the measured pace of the searches dragged the day forward from tedious to tiring to brutal. The crossing smelled of dried sweat and gasoline fumes, and the air was so dry and dusty Zev felt grit in his mouth even after taking a sip of water from his canteen. The closeness unsettled him; he much preferred the tower, his aerie, where everything was at a distance and only his rifle bridged the gap. There was no real danger here; at the checkpoint, power was made flesh—soldiers versus civilians was always a one-sided game. He looked into the faces that gave him stony acquiescence and he kept his poker face. He knew the people in line were doing the same to him. It was an identical stew of emotions in opposition to each other—soldiers and civilians each standing their ground before the formless antagonist that lurked in the shadow of every blink, every grin from the other side.

The hours went by in this way, slowly. Each side processed the other, the soldiers squeezing the men and women in line through a security sieve; the men and women from the West Bank accepting this treatment as fate, willing themselves to undergo it time and time again, week in, year out, and not change their bearing in the slightest.

Monday, Zev was glad to be back at his regular post in

the tower, surveying over the length of his rifle barrel the dribble of traffic on the road, most of it going to or coming from the checkpoint. For diversion he combed the small hills that rose on the other side of the road with his scope, watching a pair of workers in the olive trees, small packs of goats and sheep and their minders, and pretended to pick off crows as they alighted to scavenge in the trash by the roadside. It was late in the afternoon when Zev noticed movement on the shoulder of the hill, along the same path the Arab woman had run down the previous Friday.

"Hey, come look at this."

Dani was taking a break in the small, all-purpose room on the ground floor of the tower. On Zev's summons, he scrambled back up to the observation post. He shaded his eyes with his hand and squinted at the black shape, now about halfway down the hill.

"What you make of it?"

"Don't know."

"Let's see what she does. Take no chances."

Zev now took his firing position, picking up his rifle and settling his eye against the scope to watch.

It was the same woman, he was sure. But she wasn't running this time, just picking her way down the slope almost gingerly. Careful, aware—not heedless at all. Half way down, she stopped and undid her hijab. The hair tumbled out; he was sure it was the same woman now. The tresses were wild, unmistakable. The woman looked part animal, like a witch. From there, her pace got faster. She reached the road and bolted across and down toward the wall, stopping more or less where she had the last time.

* * *

It was the blankness again, yawning before her, dizzying her with its depth and expanse. It was murky, impenetrable, infinite. She wanted to scream at it, make it feel shame, make it human so it could feel pain as she did, loss as she did. She wanted it to feel its own cold vastness, its emptiness, and cringe. But it did not yield. The wall towered higher; its vastness began to envelop her. She could see only its blankness—faceless, unreadable. It drew her in. She was alone and cold, slipping toward it, into its void. She flung herself on the ground for safety and grabbed at the earth for a hold. It was too loose. She clawed at the dirt, anything for a handful of substance, but she slipped further. The void oozed around her, sucking her toward it. She couldn't see. Her hand closed on a stone and she hurled it, screaming at the top of her lungs. She kept screaming until her chest hurt, crawling for stones, dirt, anything. The grip of the void slackened and dropped off. The swirl around her calmed and rippled itself still, and into familiar shapes that didn't move. She stood up. She looked at the wall. There were a few white marks on the slab in front of her, blemishes where the rocks had struck.

The woman was laughing now. After thrashing around in the dirt, she was standing up, leaning back, laughing loud enough for him to hear. She yelled something, but the slight breeze dissipated her words, and only disjointed bits of sound floated up to where Zev sat in the tower.

She stopped laughing and glanced about; she seemed to be looking at the ground in search of something. She stooped to grab what looked to be a handful of stones. For several minutes she flung rocks at the wall in front of her, smiling, laughing, gleeful. She was crazy, this woman. Her clothes were now filthy, her hair too. That hair! It roiled around her head, whipping the air as she threw her rocks. She kept at it until she sank to her knees, her chest heaving. But she was still smiling, smiling like a lunatic.

Then her face hardened, and she began to cry. Her whole body shook with sobs, again and again, until the sobs ended. Wiping her face with one hand, she looked around and started picking up stones again, but more carefully, as if she were choosing particular ones. She placed them in a pile on the ground and stood stock still, staring straight ahead. Then she yelled something and threw a stone. She kept this up until the pile was gone. Then she stood staring for a few moments, then turned on her heel to walk away. After a couple of steps, though, she stopped, turned and stooped to pick up one more stone She hurled it at the wall with her full body rising behind the arc of her arm. The stone's crack against the concrete stung in Zev's ear. The woman stared at the wall again, then wheeled and began to walk back up the hill.

Zev tracked her with his scope the whole way, wondering what goes on in the head of a person who has lost her mind.

Chapter 5

The empty space in her class's tent didn't seem so empty any more. Aisha could teach again. The children could learn again, and they did. Her memories still lingered, filling the air under the tent, merging with each day as it passed. And the echoes of those memories would follow her each day to where she turned them into names and hurled them at the wall. Then the stones would hit the wall and scratch it, mark it, injure it, to give the void a face she could look into.

* * *

To Zev, the madwoman or witch or whatever she was had turned into yet another Arab rock thrower. They did this all the time. Every day some kid would heave a stone at one of the towers along the barrier. It was meaningless. He respected her tenacity; he had to, the way she kept coming every day. The kids didn't do that. This stretch of road was quiet; the biggest threat as far as he could see was boredom. And after the initial excitement, the woman, too, became if not boring, then mundane. Standing there, a small bit of flesh against the hulking mass of concrete, she looked inconsequential. Still, as the days passed, he began to anticipate her arrival in the late afternoon. It marked his day, and he followed her with his scope from the instant she appeared on the edge of the hill to when her wild, flapping hair receded back over it, perhaps thirty minutes later.

Every day was the same. She would walk purposefully to the same spot as the day before and survey the ground, not bothering to look up or ahead, as if she were ignoring the wall until she was ready. She would reach down and pick up rock after rock until she had a small pile at her feet. Then, deliberately now, more controlled as the days passed, she threw stones at the wall, one by one, yelling a name with each throw until the pile was gone. At first he hadn't been able to hear what she was saying, but now he could, clearly, as if it were borne straight to him on the wind—Ahmad, Nassim, Layann; twelve of them. Then she threw a last stone, a thirteenth, but said nothing, just let loose.

The stones would hit the wall and bounce harmlessly off, falling to rest at its foot, their energy depleted. When she had finished, she dropped her arms to her sides, exhausted, and stared for several minutes at the mass of concrete

60

looming over her before again turning and retracing her steps up the hillside and out of sight.

Today had been no different. Zev once again followed her with his scope until she disappeared. When he lowered his rifle, he could feel the wind on his face. It was starting to blow harder, so he put on his sunglasses to keep dirt from getting in his eyes.

* * *

The days went by. Zev sat high in his turret, watching, always through his scope; he called her Mosquito—all that stinging with so little effect. She brought the stones with her now, in a small bag. She would look at it in her hand for a long heartbeat, straighten, and yell a name. Then she would arc the stone at the wall so it hit the concrete with a sharp crack. All traces of discomfort seemed to have vanished. Zev followed the throws with his scope as the stones left her hand. Each throw had an almost identical trajectory, hitting the wall each time about halfway up its face. Her strength and aim were improving. The arcs were flatter, and the stones hit the wall harder. Her throwing arm pulled her body through the whole motion with fluidity, even grace. And Zev noticed now that, as each stone hit, a small puff of white dust would rise. Through his scope, he could see little pockmarks appearing in the previously implacable surface of the concrete.

It was mostly just the soldiers on duty in the tower who watched her. That meant Zev and Dani—sometimes another. Their shift seemed manacled to the landscape here. No new orders, just day after day of the same. And it was quiet, very quiet. Only an intermittent trickle of people passed by each day on their way to the Beitunya checkpoint. The main road was to the east. Most of the traffic going to the checkpoint took that route. Others who passed and did stop would stare at the wild figure at the side of the road for a few moments, but none lingered.

Aisha threw her stones in an intimate place she had created, with the trees of the olive grove behind as her living witnesses. Whatever eyes were in the turret remained far back in its shadowed recesses. She felt free. Not of the memory, not of the horror, not of the sadness, but of the affliction. A burden remained, but it was lighter, and there was purpose to it, where before there had only been a leaden weight of pain. She left her class in the afternoon. No one followed, though some of her fellow teachers had become curious about the change in her. She was different, in a good way and in an odd way. She seemed focused on something, something that motivated her, but that she did not share, and some worried that she had only buried her grief where it would fester and worsen, to emerge later on, larger, deeper, more toxic, more devastating.

* * *

A suicide-bomb explosion in Tel Aviv the previous day had been followed by heightened security all along the wall and at all checkpoints and crossings. No males over the age of fourteen were to be allowed into Israel until further notice. Zev had been reinforced by David Hamrash, a corporal who was assigned the job of spotter. The day had been quiet, however. Zev filled David in on Aisha, so he wasn't concerned when she walked down the hill and took her position. He studied her through his binoculars for a few moments, then panned up and down the road.

"Look there."

Zev squinted at where David was pointing, shading his eyes with his hand. Three young men, perhaps in their mid- to late twenties, were walking down the road from the direction of the Beitunya crossing.

"Keep an eye on them."

David nodded.

When they were maybe twenty meters behind Aisha, the men stopped. They had spent hours waiting at the crossing to be processed, only to be turned away. It had been humiliating, but more than that, oppressively boring. The sight of this girl flinging stones at the wall was a welcome entertainment. Almost anything would be.

Aisha stood with her back to the road, concentrating, a stone in her hand, and paid them no attention. Zev doubted she even knew they were there. He saw her close her eyes for a moment, then, opening them again, send the stone flying

63

hard against the wall. The sharp "crack!" stung Zev's ears in the tower. He could not help but wince. As Aisha moved through the names, the youths began to urge her on, their shouts carrying easily across the space and up to the observation post. All three were yelling, laughing, shaking their fists.

Aisha was still, her gaze fixed on the next stone in her hand, when the men suddenly stepped down from the road, coming nearer to her. They grabbed whatever rocks were lying within reach and began to hurl them at the wall. They went at this for several minutes without stopping, grabbing handfuls of rock, sand or sticks, whatever they could find. They started shouting, cursing the wall, the Israelis. The bursts of vitriol carried up to the turret. Zev adjusted his position and brought his rifle up, his finger braced on the trigger guard. Encouraged by their own boldness, the young men moved to just in front of Aisha and began taunting the soldiers they knew were watching them.

Aisha stopped what she was doing and watched. She did not move, but slowly took on an angry stiffness visible to Zev through his lens. Then, without warning, Aisha's rigidity melted. She rushed at the nearest of the men and shoved him to the ground, screaming at the top of her voice.

"Stop it! Stop it! What are you doing? You idiots! Who do you think you are?"

The other two men immediately stopped what they were doing and gaped at her. Zev and David each tightened his grip on his weapon and strained to hear her voice. It was hard to make out what she was saying, but what was happening was plain enough. They watched the man Aisha had shoved get up stiffly. He looked at her angrily, but said nothing.

"You think I do this for fun? Eh? You think I come down here every day just to look like a fool?"

She flung her hands up and leaned aggressively toward them. One started to take a step backward, but, seeing that his friends weren't moving, stopped.

"You think you can barge in here like this?"

"What the hell!?" one of the men managed to say. "You throw rocks. We throw rocks. Why not? Fuck the Jews!"

Aisha closed her mouth and glared at them for a few moments. The only movement in her form came from the long strands of her dark hair; they undulated around her face, stroking her cheek, which was twitching with anger. Her eyes didn't blink. The three men shuffled uneasily under her stare, trying to avert their eyes, but they couldn't.

"You think all I am doing is throwing rocks?" She shrieked this at the top of her lungs. Her eyes shrank to slits, and she shook again and again as something within her thrashed to break loose.

There was no answer from the men, only quizzical, more than a little fearful glances. She pulled one of her remaining stones out of her pocket. They stepped back, away from her intensity. She held the stone out on the flat of her hand.

"This is Ali." Her voice was low now. Quiet.

The men's faces were blank with incomprehension.

"One of my students. One who was killed."

She paused. Her voice rose again. "In the missile attack. Two weeks ago. Remember?"

The older looking of the three shook his head. The other two tried to lower their eyes.

"Shit." The brutal spit of the curse hung in the air.

"Twelve of my students were killed by that fucking Israeli missile. Some idiots like you were firing a mortar near my school. The Israelis sent a gunship, and it missed. Not that they care."

She spat on the ground. The men shuffled their feet again. Her coarseness and ferocity weren't right, weren't normal.

"I come here every day to remember. I throw the stones and pray over each one."

Their gazes broke off in discomfort.

"Look at me!"

Startled, they obeyed, and she stared them in the eyes. Hers still did not blink. They could only stare back, not knowing what else to do. She made a face, exhaling heavily, and looked down, away from them.

"What I'm doing is sacred." There was now a tired weight in her voice. "It has nothing to do with you. Go away."

The men didn't move. She abruptly looked at them

again. Her cheek twitched, and her whole body had become rigid.

"Go!"

This time each of them turned around, trying not to appear in a hurry, and walked back to the road. Reaching it, they glanced back. She had not moved; her stare was still on them. They dropped their eyes to the ground and turned away from her. Then they started again toward Ramallah. David lowered his binoculars; Zev relaxed his trigger finger. Aisha watched the men go. When they had receded to where she finally felt their disruptive presence had gone, she turned and began again where she left off, with Ali. And when she had finished, she walked back up the hill, her step a bit more laborious, her burden a little heavier today.

* * *

The next day, there was a group of seven men and boys waiting for her when she arrived. They were sitting in the shade of an old blue sedan and might have been there for hours. She ignored them and went to collect stones. When she was done, she took her position in front of the wall, but she heard scuffing footsteps and turned around. The men and boys were standing behind her.

"What the hell do you want? Go away, this is private!"

One of the men, tall and somber, stepped toward her, along with an older boy, maybe seventeen or so. When they got close, she could see how gaunt they both were. Their faces looked tired, listless, and their clothes hung loosely on their frames. The older man spoke.

"I am Ali's father. This is his brother."

He said nothing more. Aisha lowered her eyes. Her shoulders rounded as she let out a deep breath, and she nodded weakly, her body resigning itself to the surrender of her solitude. But then she straightened again, the unwanted sharing buttressing something within her. As she turned to walk down to the wall, the men and boys followed and spread out behind her in a line. They each took a rock from their pocket. Aisha went through the names softly, one by one as usual, taking a silent moment before each throw. The men and boys followed suit. Some, it appeared, had brought only one rock, and waited until a particular name was called before throwing. When it was over, she walked away without looking at them. They waited for her to get most of the way up the hill before moving off themselves, three on foot, one on a moped, and the rest in the car they had left by the side of the road.

* * *

When Aisha got home, her mother was beside herself.

"Why are you doing this?"

"I have to," was all Aisha said. She went to her room and closed the door. When Hana tentatively knocked on the

68

door later, there was no answer. Aisha was asleep.

Khalid took the news of the stone throwing with a sigh.

"Yes, I know. Everyone in the village knows. I had to pretend I knew."

To his wife's puzzled stare, he added, "So at least she wouldn't be seen as disobedient to us."

"Do you approve of this?" Hana's voice was shrill, close to panic.

"Of course not. But we need to talk to her first."

* * *

A little over an hour later, Aisha awoke, but she lay for a while in the dark before emerging. Her parents were waiting. They had prepared tea.

Aisha waved her hand to say she didn't want any, but her mother poured her a cup anyway and set it in front of her. Submitting to the familiar family ritual, Aisha added sugar herself and stirred longer than was necessary, taking refuge in swirling the liquid, the only motion in the room.

How to explain what she couldn't explain to herself?

Her father was calm; her mother was close to tears.

Khalid cleared his throat, and Aisha looked up.

"People say you should be a cricket bowler."

Aisha smiled, briefly. It made her feel warm.

"I just . . . I just started doing it. It made sense. It makes more sense each time."

"But it's not safe!" cried Hana.

Aisha shrugged.

"You can't do this! Someone will shoot you or rape you or . . ."

"I'm protected."

"By whom?" Hana stood up. "That's ridiculous! Boys and old men? Where is your loyalty to us? Do we not count? You live here but you ignore us? How do you think this makes us look? We are being humiliated!"

Khalid raised his hand for Hana to stop. She sat down. Khalid looked at the window for a moment, then back at Aisha. When he spoke, his voice was calm, low.

"I should forbid it. I should have forbidden your brothers, too."

"But you're not like that."

"No. And see what good it has done me. Us."

Aisha nodded.

"I want to do what you ask, you know I do, but I can't. I have to do this. I have to do something!"

"Isn't teaching enough? Isn't that where you are needed?"

"I am teaching. But no, it isn't enough. I don't know why. But I feel better after I throw those rocks. If I didn't, I'd explode!"

Her father nodded. Hana looked at him.

"You are letting her have her way? You need to be a father! Tell her what to do!"

"My job is to be her protector, not her jailer."

"Then protect her!"

Hana stood up and strode into her and Khalid's bedroom. She slammed the door shut.

Khalid looked at Aisha.

"This is very hard on your mother."

"I know."

"It's hard on me, too."

Aisha nodded.

"You're all we have left in some ways. Abdul is gone. He won't come back from Dubai, I don't think. He doesn't even like visiting."

"Do you blame him?"

"No. But I miss him."

"Me, too."

"Fadi, I am worried about. He visits, but he has changed so much. He's not the same."

The carefree brother who had read stories to her was now distant and disapproving. He drove a delivery truck in Ramallah and lived there during the week. It was too difficult to commute because of the checkpoints. He thought he was a scholar—everything was the Quran this and shariah that. He thought every item of clothing she wore was too tight or too short. He needed to get out more and she had told him so. He had felt insulted and ordered their father to punish her. When Khalid would not, Fadi had left in a huff. Aisha shook her head at the memory.

71

* * *

Every day, Zev counted another person in the line behind the woman he now knew was called Aisha. Some, he noticed, carried only one rock at first. They would follow her movements with their eyes, waiting for a single name. When the name was shouted, they would hurl their stones with all the strength they could muster. Then they would wait until all the names had been called and all the stones thrown, tears etching lines in the dust on their cheeks, bent over as if all the energy they had in their bodies had been in the small bit of rock they had sent flying at the wall. After a few days, each new person would start throwing thirteen stones, as if they had gained courage to make their private grief public. He watched their faces, their tears, their mouths, their eyes. As he searched the faces, his scope filled with their worlds. Dust would blow up from below as sweat streaked down his forehead. It would get into his eyes, and he would have to look away. When his eyes cleared, he would look at another face.

There were others to watch now, too. These people stood or sat on the hillside and themselves watched Aisha and the line of men and boys. They made no move to join the line. There was a space, a deference. Were they just curious spectators, attracted by the novelty or were they supporters? Zev wasn't sure. He saw wearied, indulgent smiles at first, and some derision as well—fingers pointing at the ragged

72

group tossing pebbles at the monolith, laughter. But this changed as it became evident that, whatever its original impetus, the girl's daily trek to the wall had become a ritual for her and the others, a required observance, demonstrating —no one really knew what.

The soldiers in the observation post regarded this daily occurrence with slowly mounting unease, not knowing what to do about it or what it would turn into. There were other watchers too. Two Palestinian Authority security vehicles would drive up just before Aisha appeared each day. They parked down the road, unobtrusive but hardly unnoticed. No one got out, and they did nothing to interfere, just sat in their vehicles until the ritual was over, waited for the crowd to disperse, then drove off. Their presence was noted in the tower.

The uttering of the names took on a slow, rote rhythm and resembled nothing so much as a liturgical response, almost mechanical, but bearing much that was otherwise inexpressible. The initial apprehension of the soldiers in the tower gave way to a guarded ambivalence, as it became clear that this activity, for the moment and for whatever it was, was limited to this simple quasi-ceremony: a ragged line of people led by an unhinged young woman, pursuing yet one more exercise in futility, of which this land had seen so many.

* * *

Karim Shaath usually didn't drive out of his way for anything. All that meant was more checkpoints, more delays. He liked being home for dinner. But the news had reached him, and he felt it was his duty, maybe, to at least show the respect of coming once. So here he was, in front of his past.

And it was true. They were throwing rocks at the wall.

They had already started when he arrived. He could hear the names being shouted as he rounded the hillside. He walked faster, holding himself back from running to keep some dignity. He stopped just short of halfway down the slope, close enough to see and hear easily, far enough away to feel he was remaining apart—observing, not encouraging.

The rumors had reached him first a couple of days before, at a gas station in al-Bireh, where he now lived, on the other side of Ramallah. The cashier, Abu Belal, was chatty as usual, passing along bits of information and gossip to his clients. It was a way to establish rapport, to keep people coming back. It also relieved the boredom of the job, no doubt. Karim paid just enough attention to be polite, seldom saying more than hello and good-bye and maybe occasionally grunting to imply agreement with Abu Belal's prognosis for tomorrow's weather.

"You're from Qalunya, aren't you? I think you told me once you were."

Abu Belal hadn't waited for an answer, but kept on talking, stating the rough facts for him, that people from Qalunya were throwing rocks at the separation barrier every day. A schoolteacher had started it, and now a bunch of others did it with her. Abu Belal finished by shaking his head, as if to say how strange it was how some people waste their time.

Karim got the details about the attack on the school a few days later while in line at a checkpoint. Kids dead. A school destroyed. His school. His school with the big tree. Now he was here. He hadn't been to Qalunya in a long time, not since his father died. And that was just for the funeral. The old man had wanted to be buried here, even though they had moved away long before. All the family was now in al-Bireh.

What was this about? He stood. The others were all standing—he didn't want to be conspicuous. Another name pierced, then saturated the air. The stones hit the wall again. Names of children he hadn't known. It was sad. But what did it have to do with him?

He told himself he should leave.

He looked to each side to see the clearest path out. The crowd wasn't elbow to elbow, but it was dense enough. He would have to ask people to move aside to let him pass. He felt himself hesitating. No, he was stuck. He had to wait until the stone throwing was over. Then he could leave. He straightened himself and looked back toward the wall. His feet shuffled in impatience.

Another name. He didn't hear it, just felt the sound. Then a pause, and in the silence, the air took on weight, pressing down on his shoulders, his body. Another name. Voices, stones. Voices, stones. Then no name, no voice for the last stone. The air pressed on him harder from all around. He could only take short breaths, could not fill his lungs.

And then it was over. The weight lifted. He took a long breath, deliberately expanding his chest as much as he could until the air inside him was free, unburdened. The girl walked away. People turned to leave. Karim didn't try to look at them, just let them go. He looked down at the space between the road and the wall. A strip of dirt emptying of people. When there was no one in front of him, he turned, and began to walk back to the village, where he had parked.

When he reached his car, though, he changed his mind. He would walk around for a while, to see what had changed, what hadn't. He strolled down the main street he had run so many errands on as a child and let the familiarity of this place send his mind back to when an afternoon could last forever.

As he walked, so much was the same; so many memories were confirmed. The village had changed little—a new house, a missing building. Faces he did not recognize. Why would he? The little things that helped the present dim the past.

But so much of what he remembered about this place could not be renewed, blocked from view by the wall. His house had stood in the path of the wall and was gone. His trees, where were they? Dead? Broken? Rotted into the earth?

So why had he come here?

Karim didn't know. He felt uncomfortable, out of place. He had left this village long ago. It wasn't home anymore. The community had changed. It was different, even if it looked close to the same. He had no connection to it except for his father's grave. And that was an artifact, a piece of history, not part of his life anymore. He told himself again he should leave. Yes, that was right. He should leave. Go home. Get on with things.

He wouldn't stop at his father's grave today.

* * *

Zev continued to scan. One day he caught a glimpse of a short, stocky woman pointing down at Aisha. He didn't think he had seen her before. She was talking to a man. She appeared to listen as he spoke, then she nodded and walked a little way back to a place behind the crowd, near the crest of the hill, where she squatted down to watch. Zev focused on her face, made to look even plumper than it probably was by the tight wrapping of her hijab.

He wondered what the man had told her: Aisha was a nice little schoolteacher who had given in to grief. Not vengeful, not suicidal, just out of her mind, acting out something utterly purposeless. The scope framed the woman's face. It looked a little sad, full of pity, too, he thought, as if she felt resigned to the waste he knew she saw.

But the next day, the woman was there again, well before Aisha. She went to a place farther down the hill and sat. She didn't move. To Zev she looked like a dark, pudgy rock. Aisha's arrival, always at the same time in the late afternoon, just after school let out, was expected, anticipated, and Zev saw a few people hurrying from the direction of the checkpoint to gather and wait for her.

As the throwing began a couple of the new arrivals called out to Aisha: "Good throw!" "Harder, schoolteacher!" She didn't seem to hear them, though, and other watchers quickly hushed them. After Aisha was done, the people watched as she stood a few moments in silence, straight and immobile, while the rising breeze fluttered her skirts and kicked up dust around the foot of the wall.

A pattern had emerged. Each thrower now brought thirteen stones. Aisha would call a name out; the rest would repeat the name, then a short pause in silence, and finally, together, they released their stones. The faces had changed, too. Few tears were shed any more. The people did not yell, and they did not speak other than to say the names aloud. As Zev scanned, he heard every syllable clearly, as if they were being spoken to him.

The still, squatting figure of the fat woman had settled so well into the landscape that Zev jerked his rifle around when he caught it moving, just as Aisha was descending to the wall. The woman had little, pudgy hands. There was a simple ring on one of them, which glinted sharply in the sun as the fingers carefully unwrapped the brown hijab that bound the woman's head. All the while, her eyes were cast down, looking neither right nor left as if she were in a small, private space. She stuffed the cloth into a deep pocket in her clothes and walked forward to the line, her eyes raised and fixed straight ahead. Her black hair was long, with broad streaks of grey running through it. A couple of the grey locks jumped into the wind as Aisha took her place. The woman then reached into her robes and took out a bag. Her hand went inside it and came out again, and she stood there, her fist balled, staring straight ahead. The first name was called and her arm went up like the others, and a stone catapulted from her hand to clatter against the concrete. Zev watched no one else but her. The face was not as round as he had thought, and didn't flinch as a line of sweat ran down her cheek and formed a bead on her chin. The last name was called, and after she threw her silent thirteenth stone, her face crinkled and broke, but she held back the tears, if only just. Without moving from where she stood, she replaced the empty bag in her robes and pulled out her hijab. As she wound it over and around her head, her hair, with its bold strands of grey, disappeared. Her face got plumper. She turned to leave, carefully smoothing the creases in the cloth as she walked, pulling them taut, except for one loose fold, which flapped slowly in rhythm with her steps as she walked away.

Over the next few days, more women came to join the line. Some took off their hijabs, others didn't. As each came forward, the men and boys stepped aside to make room.

* * *

Of the two men who sat in Aisha's house several days later, one gestured with his hands when he talked, and when he paused in what he was saying, tended to smile at whomever he was speaking to. Aisha had known him all her life. He was Hafez al-Masri, known as Abu Massoud, the chairman of the village council of Qalunya and a family friend. The other was more stern looking, possessed of deep, clear eyes, whose shifts of focus between Aisha and Hafez were his only movements. His body remained calm and immobile, his hands folded in his lap. His shoulders hunched a bit in acknowledgement of his status as a guest, but this was contradicted by the sharp, almost furtive glances he cast around the room. He seemed irretrievably wary, as if by well-entrenched habit. He was Nafasat Gazelah, the imam of the local mosque.

Today, however, Hafez's manner, though warm enough, was official. His voice was low and measured, as if to reinforce his seriousness.

"Aisha, we are, of course, aware of what you and the others do each day at the wall. We have come several times.

I think you have noticed that your . . . what is it, an observance, a ritual?"

He waited, out of politeness, for her to respond, and when she didn't, he continued.

"Ritual, then."

He paused again to make sure she wouldn't contradict his choice. She said nothing.

"Your ritual," he went on, speaking slowly, "is attracting attention. News cameras have come. The Authority is watching. I am sure the Israelis are watching, too. I am concerned for your safety. I want you to know you can call on me if you need anything. Any help you need, I would be more than happy to provide. I know people."

He took a long pause. Aisha sat between her parents, facing Hafez. The room was small, and made more intimate by the presence of so many unaccustomed bodies. Aisha heard the solemnity, the caring words. But she was tired, and had trouble focusing on what was said. She looked slowly from man to man and pretended, as well as she could, to listen intently.

Hafez motioned to Nafasat.

"Our imam asked to come with me. He is also very concerned about you."

Nafasat cleared his throat.

"Aisha, you and this village have suffered a terrible loss. I know you don't visit the mosque as much as perhaps you could. No matter. I, like Abu Massoud, want you to be

81

protected. And God will protect you if you let Him. If I can be of help, even just to talk to you, I will be more than glad to. I am not sure what you are trying to do with your ritual, but I can't think it will satisfy you in the end, only frustrate you."

He paused, as if not sure whether he should go on, but saw no sign from Aisha to stop him.

"Perhaps you should come more to the mosque. It also might help to wear your hijab more often. To make you feel safe. To remind yourself of your respect for God, to help you let God in to heal you. It seems trivial I know, but these little gestures of modesty and submission can comfort us, let us feel the security that God is with us at all times."

Security. Comfort. She had no idea what these words meant now and found their offers, their advice, mystifying, belonging almost to another world, to someone else's life. She no longer understood such things. She wanted to be angry with them for their presumption, for their ignorance, but whatever anger might have been trying to rise within her was suddenly gone, leaving an absence in her body. She ached and wanted only to be alone. She closed her eyes and felt the drone of the imam's voice float by her without shape or substance.

He stopped speaking and looked at her. He was waiting for a response. She had no idea what he had just asked. She said nothing for a few moments, then stood up and spoke softly. "Thank you, but I need to rest." And she left the room. Both men watched her leave and glanced at each other, unsure what was intended by Aisha's behavior and what to do next. Aisha's parents quickly filled the uneasy moment with assurances that their daughter wasn't feeling well and would they please return when she was better, in a couple of days perhaps. Hafez was effusive in restating his offer of help. Nafasat was gracious, punctiliously respecting his duty toward his hosts. He politely assured them again of his good intentions. The two left the house, speeding off in a small sedan down the narrow gravel street. Khalid and Hana, concerned, discussed the matter briefly but quietly, so as not to disturb their daughter, who had fallen asleep in the next room.

Chapter 6

When the school year ended, Aisha hugged each of the children in her class, wishing them a good summer, and told them to be ready for a great, but demanding, new grade in the fall. They nodded with serious faces, but she knew their minds were already running out the door to the months of free time in between. After the children had gone and she had straightened up what she could in the tent, Aisha walked home to long days filled with empty hours. She took out the old books from her childhood and spent her days reading them to herself. Her favorite was *Speak Bird, Speak Again*, which had been given to her when she turned eleven. She read it over and over, savoring the stories like old friends and doling them out carefully, one by one, so they would last.

In the mornings, she helped at the school. There were plans to rebuild, and this would begin soon, though they would still be using tents in the fall. Maybe by the end of the year they would have a real building again. Maybe not. She sorted books, collected materials—pens, paper, textbooks—and sifted through the rubble for whatever was salvageable. The debris of the attack would be removed when construction started. She feared what she might discover—a limb, blood-stained clothing—but all she found were books, a few notebooks, and forgotten school supplies. These she dusted off and arranged on a table for sorting later.

She also began helping her mother at home, doing chores, laughing some, little by little starting to resemble the happy young woman Hana remembered. When she wasn't helping, she was reading, and once a day she walked to the wall and back.

Hana watched each day as Aisha left for the wall, walking down their dusty street, followed by the men who had taken responsibility for her daughter's safety on this—what? Errand? Duty? Habit? Compulsion? All Hana could do was sit in a chair and wait, doing nothing, until her daughter returned.

One afternoon, as Aisha lay down her book, Hana came over to her.

"Would you mind if I walked with you today? Over there?" She inclined her head in the direction of the wall.

Aisha looked at her mother for a moment, then nodded.

"All right."

When they emerged from the house, a small group of

men who had been waiting across the street began to walk with them at a slight distance behind. Hana noticed others ahead of them. Thin streams of people were forming on the road, all headed the same way they were. It was as if what Aisha was doing belonged to their whole village. They arrived and Hana sat down as Aisha continued to the wall. Hana looked around her at the crowd. Most of the faces were familiar, though there were others she didn't recognize. What struck her, though, was the silence. And it made her feel strange, as if she were in a giant chamber insulated from the outside. Yet this chamber had the vaulted sky for a ceiling, the earth for a floor. There was only one wall, the one that stood in front of the small figure of Aisha, who had reached the road. The people in the line—there must be forty or more, Hana thought—took out their little bags of rocks. Some had been picking the ground for their stones. They stood up as Aisha took her place.

The ritual began. The only sounds were the calling of the names and the crack of stones on concrete. Twelve stones arced to the wall, borne on a name. The thirteenth stone rose in silence, and its crack lingered in the moments that followed Then Aisha turned and walked back up the hill. The others around Hana rose as well, and began to walk back the way they had come, slowly dispersing to no sound but the scuff of feet on the earth.

Hana walked back by herself. What had she just seen? Her little girl standing in front of the wall, tossing rocks at it.

A few people standing behind her doing the same. It was touching, but so futile. She sighed. The names, though. The names. It hurt her to hear them. Lost children. A waste. Children get lost. They go away with their minds, they go away with their bodies. Their parents must stay behind, and the world of nurture where they lived with their children—the love, the hope for the future—is left empty. Was Aisha leaving them, too? Like Abdul, like Fadi? What could Hana do? What could she do?

* * *

It was summer now, and dry. The wind picked up in the late afternoon, blowing dust from the hills into the valley. The wall, high as it was, had blocked the natural flow of the wind coming from the hills. Blowing down the length of the valley, it was forced against the wall, where its single column was deflected back upon itself, breaking into new currents that twisted into a writhing maelstrom—unpredictable, grasping, searching. But for all that, the wind remained invisible; only the convulsed motion of isolated shoots of grass on the arid ground between the road and the wall betrayed its passage.

In the tower, Dani and Zev watched. In his initial reports, Dani had described the growth in the crowd, and his superiors had demanded a detailed accounting of each day's ritual, with particular attention to the numbers of people who attended. This place was far from any Israeli town or settlement, but if it looked like it had the potential to grow into a violent protest of any kind, well, Command wanted to be prepared to act—with force, as they said. With force. All this meant was more paperwork—more work, period. Dani and Zev knew very well who would be set up for blame if the build-up to violence was missed. In particular, they monitored the crowd, searching, sifting for anything threatening, anyone who looked as if they would use the ritual as a vehicle for something else. Dani was quite sure that this was a waste of time and was relieved when, after a few weeks, the crowd had not grown, and no violence had occurred. The paperwork could be filled out simply, because it was always the same. Command had relaxed. The whole thing was becoming routine. As a soldier, Dani liked routine: expectations became clearer, paperwork was simpler, and stress was replaced by monotony. The ritual was a curiosity, sad, of course—IDF intelligence had reported on its origins —but far better than a mass demonstration where soldiers had to get involved. From Dani's point of view, the ritual relieved boredom and might even do him some good as the one to have reported it.

Dani and Zev surveyed the crowd together, but each did it differently. Dani scanned for odd movements, gestures, shapes that could conceal weapons or explosives. At first he had done this anxiously; several times he had seen something that put him on edge and ordered Zev to get ready to shoot.

But all were false alarms. Once it was a woman with a fidgety child, another time a man with an itch. Once it was a stray dog. Arabs don't like dogs, or so everyone said, and several men had jumped up at once to shoo the thing away. Now Dani was calm. He didn't expect anything and didn't go out of his way to find anything. Not in this crowd.

Zev watched the faces. He watched the eyes. After all this time, he recognized almost everyone there. He felt he could tell their moods, their worries, especially the women. The men were stoic, harder to read, but their faces still said much. Sorrow, reflection. There was no anger. There had been in the beginning, but that had passed. But there wasn't resignation either. Their eyes focused on each stone, one at a time, as if it were alive, with a purpose. Zev now felt he knew these people.

* * *

The coffee was cooling. Karim hadn't taken a sip yet. It would be cold soon. He didn't like cold coffee, so he drank a small mouthful.

Going to the café for coffee was his routine, a civilized end of the day after dinner with the family and before bed. A time without distraction when he could decompress from work, read the paper, be alone with his thoughts. Sometimes he'd see a friend and catch up. He had done this for years, a pleasant bit of consistency in his life.

Consistency. Today had nothing to do with that. Or maybe it did.

He put the cup down and let his mind go back to the hillside.

It was just a hill then. Just a memory now. A hill like all the others near all the villages people call home. Rocks, grass, olive trees. But he had known those rocks and trees, had run among them, played games, created adventures with his imagination. There were palaces and treasure troves on that hill. Islands in distant seas, mountain peaks. Mythical beasts and magical creatures had moved along invisible trails. And the trees had talked to him with their shade, protecting his thoughts, sheltering him from fears of growing up.

It was long ago now and his memories had broken into painted shards, each with its own scene, its own time, its own place within him—its own place in the fabric of his childhood. He had taken the hill for granted as we take all the things of our youth for granted, as permanent— unchanging fixtures to touch again and again in fact and in our minds.

Karim shook his head and took another sip of coffee. Was he getting nostalgic, longing for the simplicity, the freedom of his childhood? Maybe, but not much. No, he was a realist. He worked hard and spent his money carefully. He didn't look back and tried not to look forward too far, just enough to plan sensibly and avoid trouble. He was not a

90

dreamer, not a romantic. And there were lots of trees he could walk through in other places. The past was gone. Sealed behind concrete. Yes, you mourned the loss, that was natural, but you moved on and slowly you forgot. The present was hard enough.

He took another sip. Cold. He stood up, paid the bill and left the café to walk back to his apartment.

There was still light, but dusk was closing in. He walked on the side of the road scuffing at the dirt, taking mini soccer kicks at the pebbles in his way. He saw a slightly larger, round stone and, aiming more carefully, tried to score against a tree in the empty lot he was passing. He missed. The stone landed in the grass next to the tree and rolled back toward him for maybe half a meter. Karim went over and picked it up.

When his father had said he wanted to be buried in Qalunya, Karim had understood or thought he had. His father had been a traditional man, in his habits, in his beliefs. Worked too hard, died too young—worn to the bones. Heart just gave out. But he never lost his guts or his pride. He had wanted to be buried in the village where his family had lived for so long. To go back home. It was nostalgia, sure. A lot of the older men had done this—still did this—went back to their past in the end. Understandable. But old-fashioned.

The past was less important to Karim. He had had several homes. The family had moved from Qalunya long ago, for his father's work, of course. To Ramallah for a couple of up-and-down years, working for different, undependable people. Then to al-Bireh, where his father had opened a garage, his own business—a good business. And now Karim and his brothers ran it. Successful enough. Stable enough.

He remembered that the ground of the cemetery had been filled with stones. Stones were everywhere in this land. They were mostly useless, in the way—an obstacle to digging a foundation, to the growth of crops, of trees, even of grass. They were something to trip over, something to clear from your path. But they were part of the land, a symbol of hardship, of the difficulty of making this land yield anything at all.

In the city, you forgot about the land. The buildings blocked your view. The land became just so much dirt, blowing in your face, staining everything brown. An annoyance. Something to wipe away. He had forgotten a lot.

He closed his fist around the stone. It fit his palm. It had weight. He moved his fingers over its surface. The grit fell away, and it felt smooth, worn. So old, a piece of the land since time began. What was it for?

He could throw it—long and hard, to dent a car or break a window. Or hit a soldier. He had done that, or tried. Most of his friends had, too. Long ago, when protesting was part of growing up. Taking a stand. Becoming a man. They had choked on the tear gas, sent rocks one way to get bullets in return. Kids still did this. But he had learned. Stones weren't good against bullets, even rubber ones. Useless.

What else was a stone good for? Not much. He shook his head and dropped it. It hit the ground with a puff of dust and lay in the depression it had made in the dirt. It was part of the land once more, yet it was not dirt, not earth. It was something else.

Karim reached down and again picked up the stone. He put it in his pocket.

* * *

The seven men sat in a featureless room around a bare table. It was daylight outside, but the curtains had been drawn, and the light that entered was weak. An older man, Abu Ahmad, sat at the head of the table. They had been there for a little under an hour, going through their agenda briskly, not wasting any time. Men like these never wasted time. And they never stayed too long in one place. Abu Ahmad was speaking.

"Next item. You have all heard of what is happening in Qalunya. The girl who leads men to throw stones. I have been thinking that this girl and her actions may bear watching, but I would like your opinions."

He surveyed the other men at the table. One of them made a motion with his hand.

"Yes, Eshan."

Eshan had a long, thin face that made him look older

than the first-time father he was.

"It is odd behavior, certainly, but I think it is of no consequence. The girl is mourning the pupils she lost in the missile attack—you all are aware of this?"

The heads around the table nodded slowly.

"And the families are mourning with her. It can't last forever."

"It is an unsuitable display for a young woman. Completely unsuitable. Perhaps she needs a husband, someone to keep her under control. This could be arranged. A little pressure on her parents, and it would be done."

This came from a man called Muneeb, who sat at the far end of the table.

The same heads nodded slowly again.

Eshan spoke again. A thin smile of amusement crossed his face for a moment.

"I'm not sure a husband is the best cure for what is wrong with her. But, yes. Of course. It is unseemly, maybe even presumptuous of her. How does a young woman dare to lead older men? They let her because she taught their children. Perhaps that makes it appropriate in their eyes. In any case, it is harmless, I think."

"I think not."

Abu Ahmad frowned at the young man who had spoken.

"Yes, Abdullah?"

Abdullah al-Zahir pushed back his chair, stood up, and began pacing.

"What sort of woman does this? A young teacher, a nobody. Who is she to tell anyone what to do?"

He threw his arms up, palms open, then closed them into fists.

"She parades bareheaded and dares to lead men in this—this arrogant, pitiful little exercise! And they follow! What are they? I'll tell you what! They are unmanly, cowed, emasculated. They are not soldiers in the struggle. They are impotent! They are nothing! This is blasphemous! This is immoral! The Zionists just watch and laugh."

Abdullah paused and looked around the small room at each of the men. They returned his gaze impassively.

"She is hardly threatening the struggle, Abdullah." Eshan's smile was dismissive. "She and a few men in a small village?"

"You think not? Let me explain it to you. She is diverting people from the true path. She flouts every rule of our sacred tradition. She acts like a wild, crazy woman. This is subversive and a danger. What will she do next? She knows people will follow her now. You all know very well what that can do to a person. It makes them arrogant. It fills them with ambition, with lust for more. Yes, lust. The great corrupter of men. There are many faces of lust; this is one of them. Where is her modesty, her respect? Nowhere to be seen. She is insulting Islam! It is intolerable! It is blasphemous! She must be dealt with. She must be made to bow to the will of God. She must put her hijab back on, return to her home, and behave as a woman should, in her proper place."

He pounded his fist on the table, then recognizing that this violated the decorum of the meeting, stopped to collect himself for a moment before continuing.

He put his hands flat on the table, looked at them, then raised his eyes again. His voice took on a calmer tone.

"We will look like fools if she continues, you know. Spineless, castrated fools, hamstrung by a crazy woman. How can we command respect when we let this nonsense go on? We will lose the people. We are already losing them. Have you heard them? Have you heard what they say? I have heard the talk; it is all over the villages there. They say this is 'their path, their struggle.' Blasphemy! They will think they can abandon *our* path, *our* struggle. Abandon the sacred struggle! To do what? To follow this girl? Follow her where? They do not know. No one does. But each day they come with their stupid little bags of rocks. And each day more people watch."

A few heads nodded, a couple of others turned to their neighbor and muttered something quickly. The man to the left of Abu Ahmad stared down at the grain of the table's wood. His beard was short, and his eyes did not move. Hussein al-Waziri had no time for this nonsense. There were more important things to do than jabber over whether some girl was making a fool of herself. Abdullah was young; Eshan was soft. Both were wasting his time.

96

Abu Ahmad was asking for silence.

"That will be enough, Abdullah." Abu Ahmad lowered his head for a second, then looked up. Each man in the room felt the old man look into his eyes.

"My brothers, our emotions are often not our friends. This is such a time. And let us not confuse our own wishes with the will of God. That, my friend, is true blasphemy." He looked at Abdullah, who glared back. "Yes, she is insulting. Yes, she is out of place. But God may have a purpose for her. And let us not disparage those who follow her. They have lost much. And as far as we know, no one controls her or what she is doing. Yet."

He paused and seemed to reflect.

"I propose to watch her for a while more, without interfering. Whether you feel she is blasphemous or not— and my impression is that she is not—people are responding to her. There have even been news reports on television. And have you listened to what the Zionists are saying? They don't like this sort of protest—they like us violent, much easier to deal with. She clearly worries them. Perhaps that will help us in some way. Perhaps there is even an opportunity here if we can see it and exploit it properly. Remember, it is unlikely that the Zionists will be patient enough. They are sure to do something, and that will surely anger people. Let us not be the Zionists' excuse yet again. It is of the highest importance, however, that she not pose a threat to our position. My feeling now is that she herself has no such ambitions, nor do the men with whom she has surrounded herself. With no outside help, she will only go so far. The danger, my brothers, is that someone else—Zionist collaborators, Fatah—will try to take advantage of her popular following and use it to come against us.

"It would probably be prudent to assign a team to monitor her activities, just to make sure we are aware who may be up to what. Agreed?"

All heads nodded in assent.

"Very well. Hussein, please take charge of this."

Hussein turned to look at Abu Ahmad.

"Me? Surely there is someone else better for dealing with this." Something this minor, his tone said.

"You are detached, efficient. The situation demands that. We need to settle this and move on. There are other things to occupy us."

This was his role and had been often. Clarification. Action. The eyes that looked at him now confirmed this. There was respect, a respect that he had earned. There was also distance, the distance of colleagues who do not want to be intimates, who do not want to know a man who did what he did. Though they relied on him for it. They knew it; he knew it. But of all of them, perhaps only Abu Ahmad himself would call him a friend with any sincerity. Hussein exhaled in acceptance.

"Very well."

Hussein again focused on the grain of the wooden tabletop. He did not look at the others

Abu Ahmad turned his attention to the group as a whole.

"Now, let us move on to more immediate concerns. Hassan?"

A small man with a grey beard cleared his throat and began to speak about the progress in establishing new operational cells in the northern West Bank and East Jerusalem. When he had finished, Abu Ahmad adjourned the meeting, and one by one the men made their way out. Meetings were like this—short, in anonymous places, never in the same place twice.

Hussein made his way down an alley and arrived at a prearranged corner where his car and driver, Mumtaz, waited. He never waited long, nor did he idle in one spot. Constant motion was the rule. Hussein got in and they sped away.

Hussein noticed the time. He leaned forward and tapped Mumtaz's shoulder.

"The safe house." The voice was just above a whisper, a statement of quiet, familiar routine.

"Yes, Abu Hassan," was Mumtaz's only response.

Hussein leaned back and closed his eyes to let his thoughts emerge and debate each other. Mumtaz knew better than to disturb him. He had been Hussein's driver for over five years, as long as Hussein had been in the senior echelons of the movement. Silence was the norm. As

Hussein settled into the shadows of the back seat, Mumtaz began the circuitous route to the safe house where Hussein would spend the night, and concentrated on his driving.

* * *

The next day, in the late afternoon, Mumtaz pulled Hussein's car into a narrow alley and stopped. In the street they had just left, groups of men and women were walking south, toward the wall. Without comment, Hussein got out and joined them, turning into one more anonymous shape moving down the rubble-strewn street. Hussein stayed with the crowd, yet another man in loose-fitting clothes. He relaxed in crowds. His face was not known to his people, only to his enemies, and he felt safest as one of many, where he could not be singled out and targeted. Nor was his name known, really. He had several. His reputation alone had seeped into awareness here and there, where it was useful for it to be. Otherwise he moved among the people anonymously, not a part of them, but with them.

Hussein stayed with the flow of people until he was at the edge of the olive grove. As soon as he could see the top of the turret, he veered off to keep out of view of the observation ports. The trees were close enough together that the branches screened him completely. He looked around for somewhere to watch the ritual from and, after considering a couple of spots, chose a larger tree with low-hanging branches and sat under it, close to the trunk. He would barely be visible from the turret, but he had a clear view of the wall. He could have watched from a building farther away, or from just behind the crest of the hill, but he wanted to be closer, to get a feel for what was going on. He settled himself as comfortably as he could and studied his surroundings. The heavy geometry of the wall sat implacably on the contours of the land. He could see an area on its face that looked scratched. He assumed this was where stones had hit it. But on both sides of that, the concrete slabs stretched out flaw-free into the distance. There were no tall buildings on the other side, so he could not see what was there. It was nothingness, the edge of the earth. The finality of it had a weight he could feel on his limbs, on his chest. He didn't like this place. What point was there in coming here?

Small clusters of people had gathered on the hillside, and a thin line of men was beginning to spread out below, on the other side of the small road, just in front of the wall. A few minutes passed; then he caught sight of a bareheaded young woman walking down the far slope of the hill with a small escort of older, unathletic-looking men. She looked small, and even at this distance, the men seemed demonstrably paternal toward her. She left them at the road and moved forward. The line of people parted a little to let her through, and she took a position a couple of steps in from them, facing the wall. It loomed over her as if at any moment it could flatten her into the sand. He could barely hear her thin voice when she spoke the first name and hurled her stone, but the sound that followed, from the throats that repeated the name, came at him like the visceral roar of something caged, throwing its weight against the resistance of the wall and rebounding, filling its confined space with the concussion of its fury. Hussein leaned forward and felt the sound wash over him as each name was called. He heard the stones hit the wall. Their rhythm reminded him of waves hitting a beach, having little effect, but also inevitable, relentless. Each impact was the promise of an eternity, a vow that the stones would never stop but would hit the wall forever and grind it into the dust it had risen out of. So when the voices were still, and no more rocks clattered against the wall, the certainty of the return tomorrow and each day after hung in the air, as if the wait was no more than a pause in an unending rhythm.

The ritual over, the young woman was escorted up the hill. Hussein stayed where he was and watched the people leave, as quietly as they had come, along the road and through the olive grove, back to their homes and shops and jobs, back to whatever they had been doing before. The names kept reverberating back to him from somewhere. Children. He had no children. The death by accident of an adored young wife in his youth had smothered any urge to bring other fragile life into the world. The caprices of fate had turned against him then, and without her, a family seemed little more than a chore to be avoided. His mind darkened at the thought of putting faces to the names. Martyred faces. To be young was to be a martyr or a future martyr, by someone else's hand or by your own. Or like these, martyred by the sky itself. You died a martyr or you lived a martyr in a place where life had little to justify itself. He shook the thought away. He realized he was saddened by what he had seen. He always tried not to feel sad about anything. It was a trap to blunt the senses needed to struggle on. He fought against a long-forgotten pain rising in the center of his chest. It was time to leave this place.

He took a last look down the hill at the space filled by the line of people just minutes ago. The wall remained. Little piles of stones were building up at its foot, he could see. Pock marks dotted its face. But the monolith stood. A breeze blew dirt against it now and then, lapping at it, teasing it, baiting it. He wondered why he thought that. The remorseless impassivity of the gray concrete slabs made him shudder. He was staying too long here, taking too great a risk. Standing up, still under the umbrella of the olive branches, he turned and walked across the slope, away from the wall, using the trees as screens where he could.

Mumtaz was where he had left him, in the alley, and they drove away. As he sat back in his seat, he found himself thinking that Abu Ahmad was both right and wrong. Something was going on here, yes. But what it was, he wasn't sure.

* * *

One morning, as Aisha was opening her book, she laid it down again and on an impulse went outside. She breathed in hard and knew she needed to move. Sensations of the body instead of the mind. She needed to get out of the universe in her mind, away from fantasy. She went back inside and asked her mother if she needed anything from the grocery store, and armed with a short list and a string bag, she walked through the village toward the store. In any other town it would have been called a convenience store; here it was a necessity. Many, perhaps most, of the women around here still fed their families with food they had prepared themselves from ingredients largely supplied by local farmers. But some things had to come from outside and Bashir's store had those. It was actually larger than it had been; the village had grown and people's lives had changed. What the land produced within walking distance wasn't enough anymore, so Bashir—and now his son, who had joined him in the business—had gradually expanded his offerings. Entering the store was to straddle tradition and modernity. There was fresh meat butchered this morning, *baba ghanoush*, homemade hummus and pita, falafel and olives, local feta and *jibneh Arabieh*. Then there were the shelves filled with canned goods and a new refrigerator-freezer in back stuffed with prepared food you could find anywhere.

Aisha had been going to Bashir's all her life and knew where everything was, but she took her time, filling her lungs, her insides with the smells clashing for her attention as if they were all new. The short walk back invigorated her more than she would have expected, and as she took her purchases out of the bag and put them away, she knew why. She felt strong.

Aisha began to walk to fill the empty hours. She liked to walk at each end of the day—in the cool of the early morning, but especially after the ritual, to refill her depletion. The birds were out then, the light was rich and the air again tinged with coolness. Her village had no fixed border, no formal limit; you left the cluster of houses and walked through land your neighbors owned or worked and when you didn't know the farmer, you were in another village. Or maybe you knew his face, but didn't know his name. She passed men who were off to work and coming back from it, women on their way to the market, some on foot, some in cars or trucks. They often waved. They knew who she was. She belonged to them, was one of them, the waves seemed to say.

There are times in the cycle of the seasons when beauty hides. Beauty is so obvious, indeed so unavoidable, in the spring, when nature gushes forth enthusiastically, almost assaulting the world with its verdancy, its color. The dry summer, though, sends much of that into retreat—or oblivion —until the rains of autumn bring back the grass and the flowers. But there were little survivors, and as Aisha walked she came to look past the heat and the dust to seek out the little jewels crouched in cooler shadows, behind rocks, under trees, some opening their blooms only toward twilight, because they were too delicate for midday.

This became a game, a challenge for Aisha: to find the shy beauty. She soon grew to recognize several blossoms by their colors—lavender, golden, linen, lapis—and by their shapes—round, spiked, bowl-like, bunched, solitary. She didn't try to learn their names. She thought of looking them up but didn't. So, instead of being bound to words in her mind, the plants entered her spirit as delicate, varied emotions from the earth and the sky, the wind and the light.

The land had beauty, too. It emerged with the dawn. Fingers of shadow threw everything into relief: every tree, every stone, every blade of grass sliding, spiking into limpid air. The harsh light of the center of the day flattened it all into one dimension, features without depth, smothered by the light. But it passed. The light gave way, sharing the land with forms revived by their shadows, which moved with the current of the breeze.

Her body responded to the walks; she grew stronger and walked farther and higher. The land past her home rose quickly to the barren, unforgiving hills, high above the village, where only sheep and goats had sufficient skill and stubbornness to extract nourishment from the soil, and even they could survive only in the cooler, rainier months when the brown gave way to patches of green. The protected valleys nurtured the orchards, the fields; the exposed heights belonged to the foragers, mobile, their feet quick to move toward opportunity, not fixed in the earth.

She climbed to where the rounded expanse of the hills stretched out under the sky and she was alone with the arc of the heavens. She could see nearly forever. If she were only a bit taller, she could see the sea. This was the top of her world. Her father had once brought her up here at dusk, long ago, to look at the stars. It had been a sharp, clear night, late in the year, and it had seemed to her, as they climbed, that the universe was blossoming above them. Her father had pointed out constellations and planets, and told her their names. She had been amazed and awed with the wonder of it, but she had grown afraid of the vastness. She was small and it made her feel smaller. She had begun to cry because she felt alone, and her father had had to carry her most of the way down. But now, the sky was her shelter, infinity her friend.

The hills were bare and brown now. The summer heat had dried the grass; the sheep and goats had retreated into the valleys, which were still green. She passed their flocks in the village and on the roads as they moved to the more stubborn grass by streams on the valley floor. Up in winter, down in summer, a tide pulled by an invisible moon, impelled by an omnipotent force they could not see. Shepherds used what was there, leading their flocks to the food and shelter that

107

nature so often hid, leading them as well away from danger. Survival for them was a challenge of wits and motion. Aisha admired their craftiness, their knowledge of the land. They knew where fresh grass grew and where the way for their flocks was not safe. And the shepherds had left traces on the land, grazed fields where they had moved on, worn paths that had proven their worth over time.

Far off, Aisha could see patches of green: olive groves —trees as determined to survive as the sheep. Tenacious, both. Shepherds and farmers tending to them, at once protectors and acolytes. Farmers were nurturers, fixed to the land. They worked with the seasons and the land to create new bounty, however meager, where none had been. They changed the landscape for the future. In this land, they tended trees that were producing fruit before they were born and would outlive them by centuries. Caretakers of bounty for their descendants. It gave a robe of permanence to the land, of cycles that had always been and always would be.

This was ridiculous, she thought. Who wanted to stay on the land in any form? Her friends drove trucks, programmed computers, designed buildings. If they had a job. If they didn't, they dreamed of sparkling cities, not open sky above barren hills. What did she want? Where should she go? Or should she stay?

As she looked back down from the heights, she thought once again of stories. The ancient prophets were mostly shepherds. This made sense; they herded and guided. They led their people to safety and freedom. They were heroes and fighters. But in those tales, there was tension, a rivalry between shepherds and farmers. Which was better? Which represented the people more? Which tradition was better, stronger, more moral, more a part of the land?

The world needed shepherds, for meat, for wool—food and clothing. The necessities of life. Was that all? No, there were other necessities, other things needed to sustain life. Knowledge needed a shepherd, too. It is there, hidden sometimes, and the flock must be guided to it, and when they have consumed one bit of knowledge, they must be led to another. This thought warmed Aisha. This is what she did. She shepherded children to knowledge. This connected her with her people, her land.

But what will they do with it? Her thoughts clouded over with doubt for a long moment. Then her mind cleared. It wasn't just knowledge she was trying to teach, it was wisdom. Wisdom, though, is more like a seed, she thought. It has to be nurtured if it is to blossom and grow. So she was a farmer, too.

She looked up once more before she headed down, for it was getting dark. She looked at the stars emerging to blink across the span of the night, warm, welcoming. Infinity had a face, and it was smiling at her.

* * *

Karim had thirteen stones in his pockets and walked down the slope with his hands at his sides so none of the stones would bounce out. He had gathered them in al-Bireh, from the side streets and vacant lots, and had counted them three times to be sure he had enough.

The line was forming in front of the wall when he reached the foot of the olive grove. He continued up to the road and crossed it. The spectators were behind him now. He walked to the end of the line nearest him. A small man was getting into place. The man nodded to him, then turned toward the wall. Karim came up to stand next to him, perhaps two or three meters to the man's left.

Karim felt alone for a moment, then he didn't. He raised his eyes. There it was. The wall. Blank. An erasure of everything behind it. As if nothing there had ever been a part of him.

He heard a cry. Aisha's voice. He fumbled in his pocket and heard her stone hit the wall. The others in the line yelled the first name, and he yelled with them. Then he cocked his arm and glanced to his right. The small man stood with his arm extended, his fist closed around a stone. As Aisha's arm moved back to throw, Karim and the small man moved with her. Their arms moved, straightening over their heads and releasing at the top of their arc. Their hearts beat hard in their chests once, twice. Then came a crack, multiple cracks, as the stones hit and fell, their job done.

Karim grabbed another stone, more surely now. He looked farther down the line. Everyone was in the same position—arms cocked, stones ready. They called the second name and threw again. A rhythm took over. A name, the pause of a breath, then all the arms moved at once, lengthening, releasing. Karim began to throw harder, putting all of his force behind the stone. An energy took over him. At first it raged, an anger, but the cadence of the stones cooled it, shaped it, and he felt a strength enter and calm him. The calm remained after the last stone, and he stood with the others, staring ahead. His mind had no thought in it, and he closed his eyes. A light wind moved over his skin, enwrapped him, and he absorbed it.

The ache in his arm from the unaccustomed movement of throwing finally brought Karim back to an awareness of his surroundings. The calmness stayed within him all the way back to al-Bireh.

* * *

Hussein walked carefully back to the safe house where he was staying. Carefully, not because he was frail, not because the path was uneven, not because of many things. Hussein walked carefully for two reasons: he was preoccupied with what he had just seen, and he didn't want the wrong people to see him. Such was his life and had been for a long time. Security was second nature. But it was dangerous to descend into thought, and that's what he had done. He did this often enough; it was dangerous, but it was a part of him he could not deny. His thoughts were gifts from God, and he knew he must submit to their intrusion whenever they came. Just the same, they distracted him, and he always had to keep his presence of mind when the pull of introspection threatened to lead his awareness elsewhere.

He thought best outside. Safe houses were nearly as bad as the prisons where he had spent so many years—closed in, stifling. Safe houses were quieter, but deader. In prison you were seldom really alone, even when by yourself in your cell, if you were lucky enough not to share one. In most prisons, you shared. People were always close, always watching you. Safe houses were muffled cells of solitary confinement; the air never moved, it just settled, thick and heavy around you. Your body stagnated in them, along with your mind. So when he thought, he tried to stay outside in air that moved—in the shadows, where he could watch and not be watched in turn.

He pitied this girl; she had suffered, yes, but she was naïve. Throwing rocks is the action of an adolescent. He understood her impulse. She needed something physical, a violence, to calm her, to enervate her rage. She would exhaust herself, over and over. She had to; exhaustion was her relief, her escape. But it would become routine, then boring, then tiresome, frustrating. Her anger would grow at herself then, for doing nothing and wasting time.

What would she do then? Would she become a fanatic and strap a bomb to herself when this stone throwing proved inadequate? Would she recover or would she descend into such depths that Paradise was her only refuge? She had indeed been deranged by the rocket attack. She had lost all sense of modesty, of propriety. This could change when her rage was exhausted. It wouldn't be long.

Chapter 7

Aisha came out of her bedroom and shook the hand of the tall somber man standing next to her parents. Her father turned to her.

"Aisha, this man is from the Islamic Resistance Movement. He wants to talk to you."

He had not given his name. Habit. The name of the Movement was enough. Aisha nodded but said nothing. The four of them sat down around a small coffee table. The well-scripted proprieties of hospitality took over. Aisha's mother poured coffee for all and passed a small bowl with a few figs in it to Hussein. He sipped his coffee slowly and complimented Aisha's mother on her home and family.

Placing his cup and saucer on the table, Hussein looked at Aisha, then her parents, then back at Aisha.

"Aisha. Please let me express my condolences over what

happened at your school. Such a needless loss of innocent life."

Aisha's gaze was focused on the table in front of her. She did not move and after a moment's pause, Hussein went on.

"I was informed that you were also injured in the attack. Are you all right now?"

Aisha continued to say nothing.

Khalid interjected. "She had some bruising that lasted a long time, but otherwise she is fine. Her injuries were not as serious as we thought."

Hussein nodded.

"I'm glad to hear that."

He looked at the girl. She looked at him with no expression on her face, passive. Waiting for him to speak but not particularly interested in what he would say. He had seen this before. Social niceties often lost their meaning for people who have gone through what she had. He wondered if he was being too solicitous. Too patronizing. He wasn't good at it, he felt; maybe he was just offending her. He decided to change his tone.

"Aisha. You have impressed our leadership with what you are doing. We feel that you have become an important symbol for our people. We are witnesses to something truly wonderful. These demonstrations you lead are impressive. But as I'm sure you know, this creates a personal danger for you. We would like to offer you our help. Perhaps you would like protection, men to guard you and your house. Or you could live in a safe house, with your mother and other women, of course. We could set up one near here and get you nicely settled very quickly."

He nodded to Aisha's mother, who managed a meek smile in return.

Aisha looked up at Hussein. He put on his kindest face as he waited for her response. Aisha's parents smiled at him apprehensively.

"I can see you, you know." Aisha's voice came out softly. Her mouth had barely moved. "You sit behind that tree and watch us. Just like the soldiers, but without a gun."

Hussein stiffened. How could she see him? It wasn't possible. Someone, one of the others on the hillside, must have noticed him. He would have to be more careful.

"I'm not alone. Hundreds of people watch with me. You have become important."

"Important?" She shook her head, staring at the floor, smiling joylessly at his failure to understand. "To whom? To you?"

"No, to those who follow you each day and throw the stones with you."

"I am not important to them."

"Yes you are. You are a symbol—of resistance, of hope."

"Hope for what?"

"A future."

Aisha gave a snorted, bitter laugh.

"I am mourning the past that never became a future. I am mourning dead hopes, not creating new ones. There is no hope, and this is all I can do because it is all anyone can do: throw stones at a wall. You think it will move? You think it will suddenly go away just because we tickle it with little rocks? Or maybe you think I can blow a trumpet and have it fall down? No, the wall is our future. It is the only future, and it won't change. All that is left to do is beat ourselves against it until we die."

She took a long breath. Her chest expanded and then contracted as she exhaled. The air came out of her slowly, as if it were weighted down.

"Nothing changes. There is no hope."

"Of course there's hope, darling."

Hana touched her daughter's arm. The men remained silent, Hussein thinking, Khalid slightly embarrassed at his wife's outburst.

"Aisha"—Hussein made his tone formal, but respectful —"I have come to ask for your help. You are a leader. People follow you. More every day. I think you can help us in our struggle to rid our land of the Zionists. We would like you to be an example of our struggle, our true struggle."

She sat with her head down. He wondered if she had even heard him. He decided to go on.

"We are in a war, a war of survival. The Zionists are trying to drive us off the land or exterminate us in the process. They have been trying for sixty years. You know this. Where did your grandparents live in 1948? I'll bet it wasn't here." He looked at Aisha's mother and father.

Khalid was silent for a few moments, then looked up at his daughter.

"We do not talk about it much, not for a long time."

He turned toward Hussein and shrugged.

"What's the point? Our family's village was Andur, in the north. They came in the night, the Irgun. They blew up my grandfather's brother's house with his whole family in it. They rounded up the men and some of the older boys, those whom they could catch. Then they machine-gunned them all. My grandfather was lucky; he was away that night. He lost five nephews and cousins." Khalid stopped and shook his head slowly, back and forth. "My grandmother fled in the night with her children. They tried to come back a few days later, but there was nothing left. The whole village had been bulldozed. Their house was gone; their animals were scattered; their olive grove was gone. Every tree. It was like it had never been there. They were left with nothing. No food, no clothes, no books. Nothing left. My grandfather loved his books. My father told me how he used to read him stories at night, every night when he was a boy. Losing those books was like losing close friends. My grandfather found his wife and children a few days later and brought them here to live with his wife's family."

Hussein listened, and tried to keep from closing his eyes and sinking into memory. How many stories like this had he heard? They blended together. So many lives and practically the same thing over and over. He made a gesture to show he was moved. It was right, necessary. The common pain had surfaced again for this family. But for him the death and loss was something that repetition had smothered. He was numb now. Was he too scarred, too callused, too worn down? He collected himself and turned to Aisha.

"You see? That's what the Zionists did to us. And that's what they are still doing. We have no choice but to fight them. They are our enemies, all of them. You can help in our struggle against them."

Aisha had sat and listened to her father with her eyes cast downward. When he finished, she had brushed something away from her cheek with the back of her hand. But when Hussein spoke, she looked up again.

"All of them? The children, too? You are telling me children are our enemies?"

Hussein sighed. "It is not right to make war on innocents, of course, but they make war on us and our children. They say it is all right to kill Palestinian children because they might just possibly grow up to be what they call terrorists. And what do their children become? Their parents indoctrinate them, especially the settlers. The settlers are the worst. They teach their little boys to harangue our little girls on their way to school, calling them horrible names, vile names, names I cannot repeat. In Arabic, so the girls are sure to understand. Their little mouths spew nothing but hate. The girls arrive at school in tears. It's too much. They start saying they don't want to go to school anymore, so we have to get people to escort them. And even then it doesn't stop. All we can do is have our girls sing so they can't hear the taunting.

"What can you say about children who do that? Do you think they are *not* the enemy? What else are they? What else are they raised to be? They are poisoned with hate for us from the time they are born. Their parents have turned them into beasts, and when they grow up they go into the army and fly those helicopters and shoot those missiles. You think they care if they kill our children? They don't care in the slightest. We are dirt to them, all of us. So if you ask, are these children our enemies, what can I say but yes? It is already too late for them. They are already our enemies."

"Oh, so the Zionists abuse their children and that makes it all right to kill them? Well, that certainly clears that up."

Hussein was not used to being spoken to this way. Her sarcasm cut, and her intensity unsettled him. He did not respond.

Aisha threw up her hands and began to pace. Her parents looked on, plainly uncomfortable.

"You want my help, do you? Maybe you forget why my babies were killed. Do you remember? Or is that a bit inconvenient? Two of your men—who else's could they be?

—decided to play with their toys and attracted the Israelis, who, as usual, blasted away at everything. What did they care? The result? Innocent children dead. Nice work!"

"Those men died, too. They are martyrs to the cause of Palestine. And so are those children."

"Martyrs! How dare you! Those men aren't martyrs, they're just killers. And my students aren't martyrs, they're just dead."

Hussein tried to look indignant, but it was an effort. Her words throbbed in his mind as he tried to speak.

"That's very close to blasphemy, teacher. Remember your faith."

He heard the words come out of his mouth, but there was no passion behind them. It was the parroted script of stereotyped righteousness, and he knew it.

"Faith? Faith in what? Paradise and seventy-two virgins? Do I look interested in seventy-two virgins to you?"

He didn't, couldn't respond. He was already sounding unconvincing to himself, and her tone left him further stunned. But he felt oddly thankful nothing would come out of his mouth. Feeling stupid was better than hypocrisy.

"I'm just telling you the truth here on earth. There are no martyrs here. Martyrs are excuses. Excuses to kill and make martyrs for the other side. And all you martyr makers then sit back and claim to be blameless. That's why there are no martyrs, because no one is blameless, except the innocent. And they end up dead. My babies didn't want to go to heaven. They wanted to learn how to read."

Hussein didn't speak. He just looked at this small, intense, even passionate young woman. Her wide black eyes were looking straight into his, into him. They were deep eyes, bottomless, and they drew him in. A small horror grew inside of him. He wasn't sure what it was. He looked away.

Aisha sat down heavily and did not move. Her eyes lost their focus, and the room became silent. Aisha's parents looked at her with worried glances. She seemed drained. Her body, so charged with energy moments ago, now was listless. She stared at the floor, not moving, as if her thoughts had now left the room completely. Hussein regarded her with a mixture of anger, dismay, and puzzlement. And discomfort. He found he had joined her silence. Her words reverberated in his head, pounding at his mind. He held his head in his hands and stared at the floor himself. The two sat opposite each other, bent over, not moving. A few minutes later, Aisha stood up, turned, and walked into her room, closing the door behind her.

Aisha's parents both began to speak at once.

"We're so sorry!"

"We apologize for our daughter. She has been under so much strain."

Hussein held up his hand, and they stopped talking.

"There is no need. I am not offended. But now I must go. I will try to speak with Aisha another time. But please try to remember, what she is doing"—he paused, looking directly at each of them in turn, into their eyes, before continuing—"is dangerous. She could be hurt. Or worse. I hope you realize this. My offer of protection still stands."

Hana and Khalid nodded. Both were staring down. This was good. They were concerned for their child. And they were afraid, too, of him. This was also good.

Hussein stood up. Khalid escorted him to the door, where Hussein briefly said good-bye and got into his waiting car.

* * *

Hussein rubbed his eyes and closed them for a few moments. Mumtaz was speaking on his phone, getting information on traffic and what new checkpoints there were today. Their route was roundabout, as always, keeping to smaller roads and side streets as much as possible. They passed through one village after another, all lodged in the folds in the land, each with its own history masked by the inevitable sameness of low buildings and brown earth. Gradually the density of human occupation increased as they neared Ramallah.

The interview had been difficult. The girl was a disaster. The insults. It had been all he could do to keep his composure. The parents were mortified, of course, as they should have been. Shameful child. Wanton, disrespectful, offensive, blasphemous. What did she think she was doing? She had churned things up in him, things he no longer had time for. He fought in his mind for distance, for removal. In the little sedan, he couldn't breathe, couldn't think. He had to get out. He had to move.

"Stop the car."

Mumtaz pulled over in the narrow street, leaving just enough room for the cars behind him to pass.

"I'll walk from here."

Mumtaz nodded. It was not his place to tell Hussein what he already knew: that walking was dangerous. Hussein had taken worse risks often enough. God would protect him or not. Mumtaz pulled away and became anonymous in traffic.

On the side of the road, Hussein inhaled and exhaled once, twice, deeply, and began to walk. He was angry, and he didn't like it. Damn girl. She had upset him. He asked himself why.

Being angry was a disgrace. It was loss of self, a submission to emotion, and emotion was foreign, an enemy. It was capitulation. He realized he was walking too fast and forced himself to slow his steps again to where he moved with the pedestrians, not through them. To hurry is to make mistakes. He lived by that rule. He slowed his breathing, too. That was better. He was more in control.

He wasn't too far from the safe house, but time had shown him that indirect routes were safer, less conspicuous; he was more comfortable with the shadows and intimacy of side streets and alleys. There, time allowed him to think.

Soon he was off the main road, following the winding path of a narrow, rutted street that led to others like it. He would string them together with abrupt turns and reverses and would reach the safe house soon enough. He slowed his steps again.

What was this girl? Insulting, immature, blasphemous, yes. But he had dealt with such people before. Often, in fact. Such people were common enough, an interference, an obstacle. He knew how to sideline them, dispose of them, eliminate them. He was used to that. It was part of the struggle. So why was he so worked up, so agitated? Had she said anything that hadn't been said before? Not really. He wanted to feel pity for her. She had seen death closely for the first time, a passage he had been through long ago. Unpleasant, but a part of life, part of learning what life is really about. The violence of her grief was understandable, normal. She would exhaust herself with it and then there would be resignation. Sadness. She would go on. How much death had he seen? Perhaps too much. Death created no anger in him any more. He had submitted to it, to its inevitability. Everyone dies.

He stopped. His body shuddered involuntarily, and his muscles went slack. Then there was nothing. His anger, or whatever had been coursing through his body, now was gone. He felt depleted and stuck out an arm to steady himself. His palm slapped against flaking paint, the outside wall of a small house. All that remained was the cold emptiness he had almost forgotten. He stood, drained, trying to breathe deeply, until he knew he had to start moving again. He began to walk, and it was all he could do to force himself to go fast enough to outdistance the memories that had risen within him.

* * *

From the snipers' tower, Zev scanned down at the men and women preparing to throw their stones. The line now extended well down the receding monochrome rank of the wall. He supposed there had to be at least a hundred people standing there, ready for Aisha to arrive. The throwers were ready too, a bag of stones in their hands or a small pile of stones at their feet.

Zev still followed Aisha's movements with his scope. She was no different, her arm arced the stone ferociously each time. But now, after she threw, after the space of a heartbeat, a barrage of stones followed. The slight, sharp crack her stone made was swallowed by the torrent of sound from the impacts of all the others. Chips burst from the surface of the concrete. The spent stones lay where they landed, only to be collected every few days by the throwers and used again. Dani told Zev to let them do it, let them "recycle their empties." In addition to the stones, from the angle where he sat, Zev could see little mounds of chipped concrete at the base of the wall, a softening of the hard geometry where each slab of the wall punctured the earth.

* * *

Idith Lebrov and Miryam Banai waited patiently in Idith's car as the soldiers checked their papers. They had been sitting there for an hour. Probably they would have been better off going in the Israeli line, but they wouldn't, as a matter of principle. It mightn't have made any difference anyway. The soldiers knew who they were, and it was unlikely they would make any effort to speed things along on their account. Idith seldom came through this entry point— she normally went through Makkabim or Rantis, several kilometers to the north, which were both nearer to her home in Herzliya, a prosperous suburb of Tel Aviv—but today she was taking Miryam to see her daughter and grandchildren in Mevaseret Zion, just west of Jerusalem, and so she decided on a more direct route through the Beitunya checkpoint.

Idith and Miryam were members of Machsom Watch, a four-hundred-member organization of Israeli women who monitored IDF behavior at the more than six hundred checkpoints in the West Bank. Each day, between fifty and a hundred women, organized into twenty-four shifts, traveled into the West Bank and stationed themselves at various checkpoints in groups of two to four. Some checkpoints were permanent; others were mobile—the "flying" checkpoints— set up randomly, anywhere on the poorly kept roads that

127

Palestinians were forced to use. The soldiers, who were usually young, sometimes in their teens, by and large did not like these women, who were just as often mothers, grandmothers, and army veterans themselves.

The checkpoints were designed to choke off terrorism by intercepting terrorists before they reached their destination, but a growing consensus on the left, and even some on the right, now admitted that the main effect of the checkpoints, their main purpose really, was to harass normal Palestinians to the point where they would leave— permanently. The organization was formed in 2001 after reports of shootings, beatings and other forms of abuse by IDF personnel became alarmingly frequent. Any incidents the women observed were put on the Machsom Watch website, so that a public record was created.

Idith had joined the Watch in the same manner as many of her co-volunteers: she had grown increasingly frustrated at the impotence of merely protesting. For years, she had seen the government (it didn't matter whether they were left, right, or center) acquiesce to the building and expansion of so-called "settlements" in the West Bank and Gaza. Virtually all were illegal to start with, she knew, legitimized only after the fact. What the settlements were, actually, were "facts on the ground"—physical impediments to any peace solution that involved land. Well, now she was a "fact on the ground." To get to her station, she had to travel the side roads, the ones the Palestinians used. There were better, faster roads, but these were only for Israelis and didn't connect to anything but the settlements. The Israeli-only roads crisscrossed the West Bank and had, together with the checkpoints, turned the West Bank into a series of holding pens. Her job was to see that the people going through the checkpoints were treated as human beings, not just so much livestock.

At first, the soldiers had treated Idith with contempt. Despite her age, she had been called a traitor, a bitch, and a Palestinian whore straight to her face. This had upset her deeply. The sheer hate coming from the mouths of men, boys really, her son's age, tore at her insides. Her son had been in the IDF, too, a prison guard. The first time this had happened, she had held her composure, only to break down weeping when she relayed the incident later to the older woman who was training her. There had been sympathy, then a smile.

"Here's what I do," the other woman had said. "I look them straight in the eye and ask them 'Do you talk to your mother like that?' It shuts most of them up. One boy even came up to me afterward and apologized. But don't expect that too often. A lot of these kids are settlers' children. They have been raised to hate. They will just stare at you. Once one asked me, 'What kind of a Jew are you?' I answered, 'One whose grandparents died in Treblinka.' He had no response. These kids, the settlers' children, they know nothing, but don't expect them to change. All you should expect is that they learn to ignore you."

Idith had since learned to deal with harassment when it occurred, though truthfully it didn't happen much. Not to her, anyway. What she had noticed was that the harassment of Palestinians seemed to lessen a bit when she was around, at least the overt stuff: yelling, kicking, beating in front of Watch members was almost unheard of, though not totally unknown. Some soldiers just got more subtle, though, and that's what she watched out for the most: the whispered curse in Arabic, the "misplacing" of identity papers, the arrests for minor or imagined violations.

Idith and Miryam had spent today at the Za'tara checkpoint on Route 60, north of Ramallah. Though quite noisy with the sounds of small children, vehicle engines, and chatter incessant in the long lines, it had been, relatively speaking, a quiet day. One woman had been refused passage because she was using her cousin's identification card. She had been taken away for further questioning. An old man had collapsed from standing too long in the heat, but had revived once they had gotten him out of the sun and given him some water. Shade was a problem. There was almost none. Everyone was forced to stand in the open for the entire time it took to process them. Idith made a note to petition the IDF to set up simple shelters as waiting areas. This was a common request, and usually the IDF was quick to respond positively. Nevertheless, they always had to be asked.

There had been no incidents today. Last week a man had died at the Qalandya checkpoint, the major border crossing between Jerusalem and Ramallah, while waiting for an ambulance. A formal complaint had been made by a Machsom Watch volunteer who had been there, as the man, in his early sixties apparently, had arrived with his son, plainly in dire need of care, and had been forced to wait with everyone else for over three hours. It had been too late. Last month, at a temporary checkpoint outside Nablus, a teenager throwing rocks had been shot and killed. Another had been wounded. This occurred regularly enough and was the saddest part of Idith's job. She would see these kids milling around, waiting to be processed and she could feel the anger and resentment. She knew that it had been someone like this who had blown himself up in a Jerusalem market three years ago and nearly killed her daughter, who still remained badly scarred. A waste on all sides.

Idith was driving, staring straight ahead, lost in thought. Miryam was knitting, an occupation she had only taken up since she had become a volunteer, to pass the time. The needles clicked softly as whatever Miryam was working on progressed, stitch by stitch, row by row.

Idith slowed the small Fiat to avoid hitting several groups of people she saw ahead, standing right by the side of the road. It was a narrow, uneven road running next to the separation barrier, not great, but better than going through Ramallah, which could be a nightmare at any time of day.

131

They passed a group of teenagers, so many they nearly blocked her view of the wall. She wondered what they were doing here so late in the day. The checkpoint was several kilometers away, and they wouldn't have been going there anyway. Virtually no one, not Palestinians anyway, crossed into Israel at this hour. They must have come for some other reason. This bothered her, so she pulled over.

Idith turned around in her seat and watched them. Rather than milling around aimlessly, as most teenagers do when they have nothing on their minds, these moved more closely together, their backs to her, intent on viewing something Idith could not see from inside the car.

Idith opened her door. Miryam looked at her.

"What are you doing?"

"I want to see what they are looking at." Idith pointed at the boys.

"Be careful."

Idith nodded and got out of the car. She had long ago lost her fear of walking among Palestinians, but she never let down her guard. Suspicion was as high among them as it was among the soldiers.

She walked around the boys, who paid no attention to her, and pushed gently through another tightly bunched group of people, adults this time, older adults, also watching something, until she had a more or less clear view. She turned around to catch Miryam's eye and motioned for her to join her. Miryam slowly got out of the car and walked through the crowd to Idith and stood next to her.

What the two women could see was a long line of people, mostly men, but a few women. Most looked in their forties at least. Some could even have been in their late sixties or seventies. In front of them was a girl. At second glance, though, it was clear she was older, a woman in her mid-twenties. She was very slight and her hair hung down over her shoulders messily, as if her appearance wasn't worth even an afterthought. The young woman was shouting something, after which she would throw a rock at the wall. Then the whole line of people did exactly the same thing.

Idith turned and whispered to an older woman standing close to her, "What's going on?" The woman's eyes moved quickly to stare coldly at Idith from under her black hijab. She put her finger to her lips, indicating that Idith should be silent. Idith nodded and turned back to watch. The strange ritual, or whatever it was, entranced her. It may have lasted ten minutes, maybe twenty. Idith could not tell. But all at once it was clear that it was over. The young woman had stopped throwing stones and now stood very still, staring straight ahead. There was no sound apart from the wind, which was blowing dirt around the skirts and ankles of the throwers. Then it stopped, and all was still again. The young woman stayed motionless, just staring, for a minute or two, then abruptly but unhurriedly, turned and walked away. The people watched her go, then slowly the line broke up. The sound of low talking arose and the crowd dissipated, people walking away from the wall, up the hill behind them, or getting onto bicycles or mopeds.

The woman Idith had spoken to had begun to walk away as well. Idith went after her.

"Pardon me."

The woman turned around slowly. Her eyes looked suspiciously at Idith. But she said nothing.

"Can you tell me what that was?" Idith inclined her head in the direction of what had just happened.

"It is what we do now."

"But what does it mean?"

"We mourn our dead, killed by you."

"What do you mean?" Idith realized she sounded like a child, or an idiot, repeating herself in complete in-comprehension of what she had witnessed. She wanted to keep on asking until she got some sort of answer, but the woman had already turned and started to walk away. As she made her way down the road, her nondescript shape in black joined others, and they receded into the dusty afternoon, taking their place in the landscape. Idith felt an odd sensation of timelessness envelop her. As she watched them, the shapes were clouded for a moment by more dirt kicked up by a sudden gust of wind, but they were not obscured from view. Instead they stood out in relief against the depthless mass of earthen color that had risen up around them. The indelible silhouettes continued to move through the dry mist of dust into the distance. Idith and Miryam watched them go, then when the wind had died down, turned away from the scene and walked back to their car.

Ten minutes later, they arrived at the Beitunya checkpoint. An hour after that, an IDF soldier approached them and extended his hand for their papers.

"Corporal, can you tell me what was going on back there towards Ramallah? A group of people were throwing rocks at the wall. Do you know why?"

"The mosquitoes?"

He said this without raising his eyes from their documentation.

"What do you mean?"

He paused and looked up.

"The performance. The Palestinians' Stone Age Olympics. Little miss schoolteacher and her band of eunuchs."

Idith took a breath. Active-duty soldiers could be callous, offensive. Maybe they had to be—to survive, to justify what they had to do—but she still wasn't used to it.

"Is that what she is, a schoolteacher?"

"Yeah. Her school got hit by a missile. Since then she comes down here every day and throws stones. Trying to knock the wall down, looks like. Nut cases." He smiled too broadly. "Anyway, you can go on through now." He handed their papers back and motioned for them to move on.

"Wait a minute. We destroyed a school?"

"Accident. Some of the locals were shooting a mortar off next to it. Our guys shot back and missed. Happens." The soldier shrugged as if the whole thing were a nuisance.

Idith didn't recall hearing or reading anything about such an incident.

"I remember." It was Miryam who spoke. "About three weeks ago, wasn't it?"

The soldier nodded. "More like a month."

"Yes, it was on the news. Some children were killed, I think."

The soldier said nothing but shifted his weight on his feet and readjusted his rifle, which he cradled in one arm. It was time to go. Idith motioned to Miryam, and they got in the car. Idith put the car in gear and eased it into the lane leading to the gate in the wall. They were waved through and entered Israel.

"That's horrible! A school?"

"I'm surprised you didn't know."

"I must have been busy. I don't get to watch the news every day."

"One more tragedy. Curious what that girl is doing."

"Yes, it is."

They completed the rest of the drive in silence except for the click of Miryam's knitting needles. Idith dropped Miryam off at her daughter's, then turned toward Tel Aviv and home. Idith's thoughts, however, remained fixed on what she had seen. She shook her head to rid herself of them.

You didn't take the work home with you—this is what they had taught her—not if you were going to do your job right. Leave it on the other side of the wall. It will still be there when you return. But it bothered her, and it took an effort of will to push it out of her head and focus on the road.

* * *

The heat didn't usually bother Aisha much, but today she couldn't stand it. She lay on her bed. The curtain was closed, and her little fan was doing the best it could, but it was midsummer and heat was not a choice, it was a constant. When she was a child, she would go down to the old oak trees by the stream that ran along the road in the village. It was always cooler there, and if it wasn't really cooler, the little breeze that always was there made it seem so under the trees.

The stream was often low in the summer, and she had to lean over the grass at the edge to see where the water was flowing. The water was hiding from the sun, or so she had imagined. There were dragonflies, and she would sing to them, trying to accompany the soft buzz they made as they hovered and flitted, coming to visit her, then dashing off when they realized she wasn't a flower. She used to giggle at that, fooling the dragonflies. Her songs were nonsense— made-up words and jumbled tones. She wasn't trying to make sense, just join in the music around her, add her sounds

137

to the wind in the leaves, the rustling of dry grass, to the birds that chirped and shrieked, and the insects that whirred and crackled.

Now she lay in the dark with the curtains closed. The only music was the buzzing of the little fan. Its artificial breeze wasn't cool, but at least it was moving. Without it, the heat wrapped around you and you started to breathe faster and faster to get enough air. And all that did was make you hotter.

She just wanted to lie where she was until it was cooler, but she knew she had to go out into the heat soon. She had to go out to the wall. The compulsion had become a chore. There, she had said it. Not out loud, but to herself. But she had to do it. She was expected there. People were waiting.

She rolled her head from side to side to get that thought out of her head. No, that wasn't it. They weren't necessary. She didn't need the others. Some days she appreciated that they were there, being supportive. Some days she just wanted to be alone. Today she wanted to face the wall by herself. She wanted to ask it why she was there. But it wouldn't answer her. It had no voice, no tongue. Just a presence that glowered down at her and taunted her. It pitied her. She knew that's what it was thinking. It pitied her frailty and laughed at her little rocks. They tickled. It had no eyes, but it knew she was there. Someone was doing the tickling. She felt a burst of heat from within her. Its arrogance made her angry. She felt a drop of sweat slide down her cheek. She was so hot. The weight of the heat pressed on her. It pressed on the whole world. She was insignificant. She wiped the sweat away with the back of her hand, and closed her eyes tightly to squeeze back a tear.

The wall ignored her. What did she need from it? Why did she go back, day after day? Did she want it to open its eyes for once? And what would it do then? It would grow a mouth and laugh. Yes, that's what it would do, she was sure. It would laugh, and the laughter would break over her again and again. Unceasing, a tide of nature. Relentless and permanent. It would tumble her away. She smacked her hands to her ears to smother the sound. With her eyes closed, she stiffened her body to resist the pounding and waited until she was sure every snort, every chortle, every giggle, had stopped. Then she waited some more, until she was sure the echoes were gone, until the resounding of the laughter had ceased to shake her room, her body, her mind.

"Aisha! They're waiting outside for you!"

Hana's voice chased away the last, faint remnant of the wall's assault.

"Aisha!"

Aisha opened her eyes and sat up. She exhaled, and her breath felt hotter than the room. It took all her focus to put on her sandals, but as soon as she did, she found herself outside, walking toward the wall. The men who walked with her spread out and gave her space, then followed behind.

Her stride and pace were rote. The time was for calming,

139

for the assembly of purpose as the wall drew her to it. But today she looked around. A breeze tempered the heat. She wondered where it had come from. From the stream? Was it dry now? Probably. The motion of the air eased her along. A little girl stood in a doorway to her left. Almost school age. Aisha smiled and waved. The girl raised her hand to wave back, but stopped, unsure. Then the hand began to rock from side to side and there was a little smile back. School would begin in a little over a month. A question flickered: Would Aisha have the girl in her class? Her open palm clenched into a fist. She wouldn't let any more thoughts in. She wouldn't.

Aisha blocked out everything now by listening. She heard her sandals scratch on the dirt with each step. It grated on her ears, but it was a rhythm, and she quickened her step a bit to ease into it better. There, she had it. She heard the dissonance of the steps of her self-appointed bodyguards as they shuffled faster to keep up. She wanted to smile, and she did, but just to herself. No. No more thoughts. She opened her mind and surrendered to the sounds around her.

This time of the afternoon, the birds were quiet. It was too hot. Sensible birds. The breeze was keeping the flies away. All she had was her steps, measured, taking her to the wall. She entered the olive grove and took the path around the side of the hill. The wall began to come at her. Its form slid into view as she rounded the curve of the hill; then it rose as she descended toward it.

She couldn't hear her feet any more, though she could

feel them dig into the ground with each step, slipping now and then on the loose earth. She reached the flat and crossed the road. When she reached her spot, she stopped and raised her eyes to the wall. It could not see her. It could not hear her. It was just there. Immovable, immutable.

She felt the heat reflecting off the concrete press on her face, again and again. A little breeze, cooler and choked with dust, chased the heat away. Only little sounds remained. A foot scratched the ground. The intake of a breath. Hers.

It began. The strikes on the wall turned into music. The cries of the throwers, then the beat of the stones. The rhythm lulled her, and she was aware of nothing but her motion and the melody it made. Her body was fluid, limber. Legs set, torso curved, arm bent. The shout, then the release and the brief moment of suspended emptiness before the stones struck, and the song of the stones rose back to her. A wordless song. It was nonsense, and she knew it. But she closed her eyes and let the stones sing to her.

The song of the names alternated with the song of the stones until the last silent arc ended in a note that resounded down the line. She stood and listened to its path up the line, away from her. After a moment, the wind brought the echoes of the distant strikes back to her, and her face felt the caress of the air as the sound enveloped her, then faded as it sank into the earth at her feet. She stood in her place as the stillness rose and overcame her. The wall was not laughing at her. It had no mouth to open wide, no eyes to crinkle with

141

mirth. Dumb, stolid blankness was all she saw. Aisha turned from the wall, shunning it, and let her memory play the music again.

The walk back home took no time. When she got there her mother was in the back, looking at the tomatoes she had planted late in the spring. When she noticed Aisha, she turned.

"Look, Aisha. I've never seen anything like it. So many buds. We're going to have lots of tomatoes this year. Isn't that wonderful?"

Aisha stood beside her mother and nodded.

Chapter 8

There was an odd smell in the house. Hana followed it to Aisha's door.

"Aisha? Are you there?"

A pause, then, "Yes."

"What is that smell?"

Hana heard movement and the door opened.

"Aisha! What happened? Who did this to you?"

Hana rushed to gather her daughter in her arms. Aisha began to cry. Hana led her to the couch, and they sat down. The smell, which now filled the small living room, was burnt hair. Aisha's long, full tresses were ruined. Ragged strands clung to her shoulders; much of the hair on one side of her head was a foot or more shorter than the other.

"I'm all right."

"No, you're not. Look at you! Who did this?" Hana

143

repeated.

Aisha shook her head, and threw her face in her hands. She began to cry again.

"I was just waiting for the stars! I just wanted to see the stars!"

Hana put her arm around her daughter, pulling her close. The room throbbed with Aisha's convulsive weeping; Hana clung to her tightly as if Aisha might buck her off. Gradually, the heaving lessened, and Hana could relax her grip. Aisha wiped her face with her shirt.

"I didn't hear them. I was just looking up. Right above me was very black, and I tried to count the stars as they appeared. Then someone was on top of me beating me. They started calling me names, horrible names."

Her chest moved with a muffled sob.

"Why do they do that? Why do they have to call me names? Isn't beating enough?"

Aisha touched her cheek. Bruising had started to appear. A purple stain was spreading over one side of her face.

"How many?"

"Three, four. I don't know. It was dark. I couldn't see. The only light came from their cigarette lighters."

"Cigarette lighters? What? Oh!"

"They held me down and grabbed my hair and tried to light it. Another played with my breasts and tried to stick his fingers in my crotch, but he couldn't. I bit his arm. I was kicking and biting them, so one had to sit on me. He stared right at me. I can't get his face out of my mind. He was so angry. He spat on me and slapped me, called me every disgusting name he could think of. Hebrew and Arabic."

"So they were settlers."

It wasn't a question. The nearest settlement, Kiryat Eleazer, was more than ten kilometers away, but the previous year a group of men from the settlement had set up an outpost on a hilltop maybe three kilometers away. They had begun to erect permanent structures almost immediately, but the Israeli authorities had intervened and bulldozed them all. Afterward had come the "price tag." A small gang from the settlement had gone on a spree one night, badly beating up two shepherds, a father and young son, and killing most of their flock of sheep. There had been no arrests, and the memory was still raw in Qalunya.

Hana's face clouded over.

"Aisha, did they rape you? You have to tell me."

"No. They wanted to burn me. One of them pulled at my hair, and I screamed. He pulled again and put his lighter into it. He yanked away a few handfuls of burnt hair, then he yelled and dropped his lighter. He must have burnt himself. I got an arm free and scratched the face of the one sitting on me, and he jumped off so I was able to stand up. I kicked him and just started running."

She laughed suddenly, contemptuously.

"They couldn't catch me."

"They chased you?"

"Oh, yes. But it didn't last long. They stopped after a couple of hundred meters. I could hear them try to curse me. They sounded like wheezing old men!"

She laughed again. Then she sagged, exhausted.

"I need to lie down."

"First let me look at you. Do you think you need to see a doctor?"

"Not tonight. I'm tired. I just need to sleep."

Aisha went into her room and lay down. But as soon as she closed her eyes, she opened them again. The voices were clawing at her, drawing her down into the void. She heard them still, cursing her, reviling her. "Filthy Arab whore! This is holy land, our land! You defile it with your stench!" The words hit her like cudgels as the fists battered her to the ground. "Bitch, get off our land. Get off our land!" She twisted and writhed as before, when they had kicked her as she lay in the dirt and fingers had grabbed her hair, raising her head up to burn her. But she could not bite or scratch to turn the voices to squeals and run away into the night. She could only widen her eyes against the voices as they tried to pull her down, deeper and deeper into the void. Nothingness began to close around her. She thrashed on her bed, trying to turn her head away from the sound, but it came from all sides. She allowed herself to blink for an instant and stared hard upward into the blank ceiling, forcing her eyes to stay open. And as she strained, the ceiling faded, and the infinite night sky grew over her. The pull of the void weakened, and as the stars brightened, the sky smothered the voices with its light.

* * *

The doctor confirmed the next day that, aside from the bruises on her face, which looked worse in the daylight, she was all right. She would be better in a few days. There were no broken bones. She had a slight burn on her neck and he gave her some cream for it. She was very lucky, he said.

Her mother urged Aisha to wear her hijab to cover the damage to her hair and face; Aisha refused. Her father insisted they file a report with the Civil Police, and he and Aisha spent several hours in Ramallah filling out forms and having a police doctor examine her injuries. The police were sympathetic but confirmed that little could be done without positive identification.

"Like any crime," they said.

Khalid would not let Aisha walk to the wall for the ritual and, defeating her protests with paternal stubbornness, drove her there instead. She was moody and silent the whole way. As soon as she got out of the car she was surrounded.

"What happened?"

"Your face!

"Who did this?"

The men looked at Aisha gravely, some muttering to each other, while women swarmed around her, barraging her with questions, feeling the singed ends of her hair, weeping with shock at her damaged face. Khalid, who remained standing by his car, found himself the object of expressed sympathy for what had happened and unspoken disapproval for letting Aisha walk around the countryside unprotected.

Ahmad, a neighbor, came up to him.

"Did the Civil Police say anything useful?"

"Not really. They said we could file a complaint with the Israeli police as well."

"What are you going to do?"

"Aisha knows she was lucky. If she wants to walk around, she'll need to stay closer to home."

"Will she listen?"

"What do you think?"

Ahmad nodded in acknowledgment of the difficulty of having a headstrong child.

"It's hard not to be angry sometimes." Khalid said this to no one. Ahmad nodded.

The ritual proceeded. An exasperated Fadi greeted them outside when they returned. Aisha went inside to her room, where she collapsed, exhausted. Khalid and Fadi remained outside, where Hana could not easily hear them.

"Father! You actually took her down there? I can't believe it!"

Khalid sighed.

"Your sister insisted on going. She is committed to it."

"Forbid her! You are her father. Tell her what to do. She

has to obey!"

Khalid smiled.

"Just like my sons do."

"She's a woman. That's different. She must not do this. She looks crazy, her hair uncovered, dressed the way she does. And now this disgrace. She was almost raped! She is dishonoring our family. What kind of father are you to allow this?"

"You need to calm down, Fadi. And until you are a father, perhaps you should hold your tongue."

Fadi knew enough to let it go at that. Hana asked him to stay for dinner. To please her, he accepted, but he left as soon as the meal was over.

* * *

Today was Tisha B'Av, so Zev hadn't been able to get drunk last night. He would make up for that tonight. All afternoon he had sat up here; nothing was moving anywhere except the flies above his head in the turret. He had killed about a dozen with his logbook, but the numbers hadn't dwindled. Where did the damn things come from? Wasn't there enough garbage in Ramallah or one of these little shit-hole villages to keep them busy?

A figure appeared in the olive grove, making his way toward the wall. Here it was again. Zev watched the man make his way among the trees, fanning himself once or twice with his hand. Hotter than hell out there today, and these idiots still keep coming. Zev sat up and reached for his rifle, which was lying on the built-in table beneath the turret's opening. He set it up, but didn't hurry. He knew the drill. No sense breaking a sweat; he had plenty of time.

A few more figures appeared, and Zev began to scan them. He recognized just about all of them—the early birds coming to get the best seats. He yawned. He poured some water into his hand from his canteen and splashed it on his face. Then he took a drink. Damn water was hot. Too late to go downstairs for some that was colder, the hillside was filling up. He put his eye to the scope again. Same faces, exactly where they were the day before. Same yelling, same clatter of rocks on the wall. A rhythm he couldn't get away from. Like the refrain to some stupid pop tune he'd get stuck in his head every now and then. But this was every day, banging at his mind. He lifted his head and leaned into the scope again. He decided to trace the crown of the hill. The trees stood by as men and women walked past them. Zev wondered what the trees thought of all this. Were they annoyed at this intrusion into the olive grove? All these people. Did all this activity interfere with the hard work of ripening? Did they want to be left alone? He did. He scanned from right to left across the hill, alternating trees and people. He could see olives clustered on the branches, beginning to weigh them down. He liked olives but it was too hot to feel hungry. Thirsty was different, and he began to think of the first beer he was going to have after his shift was over.

He stopped. There was something weird about the tree he was looking at. He squinted and upped the power on the scope. And there he was—or rather it, an opaque shape that he knew was a man. Beyond that he couldn't really tell much; the tree's foliage was low and dense, and the man was in shadow.

Why was this guy hiding? Who was he? Zev forgot his thirst and spent the next few minutes peering as hard as he could at the figure. It didn't move. It may as well have been made of stone. Or wood. Wood fit better. A profile carved into something once alive but now dead. The clatter of the stones on the wall pulled him back to his job, and he switched positions to scan the throwers and the crowd again. When the ritual was over, he yanked the scope back to the tree with the shadow man. He wasn't there. Zev checked the neighboring trees to make sure he hadn't made a mistake. Nothing. All he could see was the backs of those walking away from the ritual. He yanked his scope from figure to figure. One of them had to be him, but there was no way of telling. Fuck!

Over the next few days, Zev hunted. Now he had something to do. To hell with little bint and her fan club. He had to find out why this guy didn't stand in the sun, exposed like the rest. Zev liked to think he, Zev, was the reason. The man was wanted. That had to be it. He couldn't afford to be noticed. But he was here for a purpose. Those types didn't waste their time. So, should he shoot him? He couldn't miss, not from this range. Kill a wanted terrorist, that would get him out of here, back into real active duty, not this shit.

But he kept missing him. He saw him there, but he came and went with the crowd, using the trees as cover. Zev watched the tree. He ignored everything else. And still every day was the same. The shadow wasn't there; then it was. The man had chosen the tree well.

* * *

The mirror had hung in Aisha's room since she was a child —a birthday present for a teenager, with a twisting frame of dark wood. She used to preen in front of it before school— adjusting her hijab so it fell exactly right, combing her hair, experimenting with make-up, which was expensive and thus every gram had to be used for maximum effect. When had she last looked into it? She couldn't remember. But she did now. Aisha fingered the shriveled ends where the fire had touched her hair, holding them to her face. She avoided her own eyes. She didn't want them staring at her. Applying make-up had been a secret pleasure that she could do for hours. The bottles and cases, most not used since their novelty had waned, were in a drawer. The surface beneath the mirror was bare except for a comb and brush. She picked up the brush and held it, searching for someplace to start. She avoided the damaged areas and went first to the longer strands.

Aisha had neglected her hair these weeks, and it reprimanded her by snagging immediately. The bristles could barely penetrate to do their job. She tried harder, and the clumping and matting loosened under the pressure. Once or twice she had to put down the brush and pull apart a snag with her fingers, trying to be gentle. As she got closer to the damaged area, she grew more tentative. Would she make it worse by touching it? She took one of the withered strands between her fingers and stroked its length. It was crinkled and brittle. The tip broke off, and she held it for a second, again feeling the heat of the lighter's flame against her face, seeing its flicker from the corner of her eyes. Aisha discarded the tip; the damage was done. She brought the brush up and pulled it down the damaged side of her head. She could hear faint cracks as more pieces broke off, but she stroked again and the hair began to look better. The snags gave way, one by one, as the hair began to accept the brush. She pulled down, stroke by stroke, until her hair fell as she remembered. The missing pieces were there in her memory, and she slowed her strokes as if to replace the shriveled ends with their previous length. Then she returned to the present and stroked what was left. Stroke by stroke, the hair flattened and submitted.

When Aisha finally replaced the brush on the table, her hair shone, ragged as it was. Even the damaged side seemed to have gained a little bounce, a promise of eventual restoration. One of the shortened locks touched her cheek. Aisha began to twist it around her finger and raised her eyes to the mirror. The eyes that met hers narrowed and fixed straight at her. She tried to hold them, see what they could tell her, but she couldn't do it for long. She glanced at the brush. It was full of broken bits of her hair. She grabbed it and pinched the hairs out with her thumb and forefinger. This took a while and when she had them all in a little pile, she took it and rolled it into a tiny ball in her palm and dropped it in the wastepaper basket under the table. She looked at the brush. There were still a few little burnt hairs caught in the bristles; she doubted she would ever get them out. She raised her eyes.

The mirror's eyes met hers again. This time they didn't stare. They moved—tracking the outline of her face, reading it, learning from it. The eyes would stop here and then move on. What were they seeing? She wasn't sure. The skin crinkled in new places—summer dryness—had to be. It was flatter, too. Pulled tighter over the frame of her jaw, her temple. Not a lot, just enough to be noticed, to be a change. Aisha took her index finger and touched her mouth. In the mirror, the finger was in the center of the woman's lips. It found an opening and felt the hardness of her teeth at the same time as the softness of her flesh. A line had appeared at the corner of the mouth. Aisha moved her finger to feel it on her own face, but the skin felt smooth. She saw the finger trace the curve of her cheek down to her chin. Then it fell away.

Aisha took another long look at the woman facing her. The woman was searching Aisha's face. What for? What was the woman finding? It will take a while for me to become familiar to her, Aisha supposed.

* * *

Idith began to attend the ritual as often as she could. Each time there seemed to be more people watching—younger ones, especially, and more women. There were women in the line too, now. The shock at seeing the young teacher's injuries had passed. The swelling had gone down in a couple of days and the bruises had yellowed and faded. The damaged hair still flew out behind the girl crazily, but she, if anything, looked saner, more determined. Idith never saw her speak to anyone or even acknowledge that anyone else was there. When she arrived, the crowd had already formed. They let her through to take her place in front, and when she was finished, they stepped aside to let her pass, to walk back up the hill. Idith did notice that a group of men followed her as a sort of bodyguard. Yet they were older types, and Idith guessed that they were fellow schoolteachers, or relatives, or friends, certainly not anyone capable of protecting her should anything serious happen. It was more like a paternal gesture, something you did for someone you cared for—well meaning, but hardly professional.

155

It occurred to Idith that this ritual could not remain unnoticed. Surely the soldiers in the turret were reporting everything to some anonymous office in Jerusalem, and she began to be aware of a couple of small groups of men who stood back, watching. Some were men in the uniforms of the Palestinian Authority security services; the others, she was unsure of. None of them did anything but watch. She wondered how long it would last.

One day a television crew from Tel Aviv set up a camera on top of their van and filmed the ritual. Afterward a woman reporter and a cameraman ran after Aisha to try to interview her, but the men who walked with Aisha shooed them away. The reporter then had herself filmed with the wall as a backdrop. When Idith watched it later on the news, the camera zoomed in to show the speckling of little pockmarks, and when it zoomed out again, the pockmarks seemed to be sucked back into the wall's gray, looming mass.

Idith now took Route 443 back to Tel Aviv fairly regularly, entering Israel through the checkpoint at Maccabim. She felt like a hypocrite doing this; Palestinians were effectively barred from using it, but the alternative was to drive on the Palestinian roads and wait for at least two hours before she could pass through. And to tell the truth, after a day at a checkpoint, sitting neck-deep in cruelty that at any moment could splay into violence, all she wanted was to get home. With her Israeli plates, fewer questions were asked, even if sometimes she was fairly certain she was being made to wait longer than others just because of who she was. The identities of Machsom Watch personnel were well known to the IDF, and she had no doubt that even though Machsom Watch did not monitor the crossings into Israel, the soldiers here harbored the same resentments as their fellows at the interior checkpoints.

She could have crossed near Jerusalem and taken Route 1 to Tel Aviv, but the traffic on Route 1 could be bad, and in any case she wasn't comfortable being in or even near Jerusalem much these days. The air bothered her. She liked the dryness of the hills better, and the scents that perfumed the road when she drove. She liked the hills themselves well enough, they were beautiful and rich with history, but they weren't home; to her they weren't Israel. No, that wasn't right. The hills were Israel. It was Jerusalem that wasn't. Not *her* Israel. Not anymore. She just couldn't breathe there.

Typical Israeli, she thought, conflicted about everything, especially her country and her loyalties. To outsiders, Israelis closed ranks and said they would settle their differences themselves, except that they never had—not since Moses anyway—and she couldn't believe anyone was fooled. A nation of contradictions and hypocrisy. Just like taking this racist road because it was a faster way to get away from the racism of the Occupation. Nothing made sense, even the word "Israel." Was this a country or a concept, the rebirth of an ancient kingdom, a claiming of an ancient right? What was this country? She shook her head. She had no answer, and didn't trust those who said they did.

Her Israel was Tel Aviv, where the air was humid and the sensuousness of Mediterranean living filled your head and your lungs just by the unconscious action of breathing. You could practically touch the difference. Tel Aviv was vital, active, full of entrepreneurs, late night cafés—life! But it wasn't so much that Tel Aviv was exceptional, no—it's just that it was, well, normal, as normal as an Israeli city could be anyway. In Tel Aviv, yes, it was ninety percent Jewish, but it was nonetheless very cosmopolitan, and you didn't feel you had to declare your faith every other second. You happened to be Jewish; you happened to speak Hebrew. It was less stressed. People went to the beach, for God's sake!

Jerusalem, well—Jerusalem was something else again. How did she feel about Jerusalem? Her daughter had lived there for a while, until she emigrated to the U.S. with her family two years ago. Her husband wanted to live in California, anywhere but here. Idith missed her daughter acutely but didn't blame them for going. She had visited the young couple often for the few years they had lived in Israel, playing babysitter for her two grandchildren, who were now school age. She had never felt safe in Jerusalem, and hadn't felt comfortable letting her daughter raise her babies there. It wasn't the Arabs so much either—it was the tension. Too many passions in the air, she supposed, too rich a mix, always on the verge of explosion at the slightest spark.

Was Jerusalem a city or an emotion? Reclaiming Jerusalem for Jews was a defining purpose for most of the Israelis there, a battle of birthrates and zoning codes. Two-thirds of the people in Jerusalem were Jews, the rest were Muslims, with a few Christians. The old city, though, the emotional heart of Judaism, was ninety percent Muslim. It was a museum, beautiful but forbidding, its history ponderous, a weight on one's soul—on hers anyway. For her there was something oppressive about Jerusalem that got heavier and heavier as one approached the Temple Mount. Maybe there was simply too much history, competing histories really, for one soul to bear by itself.

It was the wall, she thought, the Wailing Wall, the *Kotel*, the last remnant of the Second Temple, destroyed by the Romans in 70 C.E., when they cast out the Jews for almost two thousand years. Or that was the story. She had been to the *Kotel* and seen the lines of people waiting to touch it, pray before it, become intoxicated with their proximity to what had once housed the holiest of holies. It was a tourist site, of course, but among the inevitable hoards of tourists there were men praying, not for show but really praying, off in another world or time, their faces inches from the stone, their heads bobbing up and down—*davening,* as they expressed their love for their God with "all your mind, with all your strength, with all your being," as the Torah says—

mouthing the silent words that paved their journey to wherever it was the prayers took them. A good many were old, dressed in black, the haberdashery of devotion, and as often as not you could see tears streaming down their faces as they remembered and grieved.

Where were those men, really? With their antiquated clothes and ancient mutterings, they didn't seem to be living in the present. Were they transported by their incantations back in time to the height of the kingdom of Israel when the temple stood alone on the Temple Mount, sharing nothing with foreign faiths? Did they descend into history to bathe in the glories bestowed by God when Israel had had His favor? Idith did not doubt their sincerity, but she wondered, were they praying to the timeless, to the eternal, against whose march no wall could stand for long, or were they just praying to a cherished lost antiquity, a memory of something forever beyond reach, yet gilded enticingly by centuries of longing? Old men seeking solace, flailing against regrets and lost hopes.

Others were younger, not in black, and wore the *kippot s'rugot*, the crocheted *kipas* of the fundamentalist settler movement. These faces did not weep; they moved in prayer with features so frozen with intensity that they mimicked the stone. They were remembering too, but not to grieve; they were remembering, rather, to stoke their being with the fire of vengeance. She could see it rise within them and recalled their resolute stiffness as they stood there. She had hoped to see the release of tears that would give at least some sign to her that they had surrendered to God. But there was nothing, just a cold determination mined from the depths of time. She also wondered what they prayed to. It was not a God she knew. The thought made her shiver despite the heat.

The tourists, for their part, usually hung back, intimidated by the intensity of the faithful and hesitant to approach the holy blocks of stone, as if, being of only mortal flesh and bone, they were too fragile to come into contact with such holiness. So the scene was always dominated by the silent motions of men. There weren't many women at the wall usually. There was a fence to separate the sexes. Men and women were not supposed to pray together. And of course the space for men was much, much larger, as if the faith of women were of a lesser grade. At least that was Idith's reaction.

Her Jewishness drew her down to the wall, though. She felt something when she was there—sadness at the destruction of the temple so long ago—and she mourned the losses of her people before and since. It was a holy place, an ancient place. But it was also a place where people stood with their backs to the present and intoned to a towering mass of pitted, ruined stone, looking into it for the glories of the past. But it was not a good window on the future.

Maybe she should have gone to America with her daughter. No, that would have killed her husband, Ari, a proud Sabra who had grown up on a kibbutz in the north. So she had stayed. But she stayed in Tel Aviv, the Israel of the present. She had joined Machsom Watch when her son had come back from his service in the army and described enough instances of abuse to shock her to the bedrock of everything she had thought she knew. He wanted to leave too, he thought, maybe, but he would finish university first.

She turned her attention back to the road in front of her. She had crossed back into Israel and was descending toward Tel Aviv and the coast. Here the vegetation grew more lush on the side of the highway. The air was already more humid and was heavy with the smell of the sea. Idith could feel her pores open to the moisture, alleviating the dryness that the mountains always inflicted on her skin. The terrain flattened, and she began to relax. Tel Aviv was new, founded in 1909, only a century old, though with plenty of history already, a lot of it not very pleasant. The excesses of 1948 never left her consciousness, but at least here was motion, forward motion. Maybe it was the sea, the rhythms that never stopped, never let you freeze at one place in time. The sea would annihilate all edifices of pretense put in its way. So did the wind, she corrected herself, but it was more subtle, eroding the old as it caressed the new. The wind was here too, blowing up from the water, carrying what moisture it could to the mountains, drying out, releasing rain to sustain the pastures and olive groves, then continuing over the peaks and down to the desert. Yes, the wind carried life. She smiled and felt its warmth renew her as she drove.

162

As she entered Tel Aviv's city limits, the traffic thickened and she had to slow down. Her mind turned to the young schoolteacher. She wondered how long she would keep it up, whether she would exhaust herself in its pointlessness or would push too hard for someone else's taste. She feared for the child.

Chapter 9

It was high summer and work at the school had stopped. Aisha's routine simplified. Home, wall, hills. She strode to the ritual; she wandered the hills. At home she performed the chores of a daughter, of her childhood, helping her mother in the kitchen and with errands.

The days passed with the rhythm of tides. Aisha rode the flow between the wall and the hills. Ebb and flood. The pouring out and soaking in. Sorrow and joy. Pain and succor. Dark and light. The void and the fullness. Each pulled; each pushed. The cold depths in the concrete against the intimacy of the sky.

She was at home when she wandered, with the arc of the heavens above her and the soil it sheltered firm under her feet. The outpost was gone, bulldozed by soldiers. She would cross the tread marks, and saw them flatten under the ceaseless wind as the hilltop restored itself.

The sky and the land it sheltered held her against the pull of the void. As she squeezed each rock in her hand, the coldness reached out to her from the wall and for a moment her head became light and she might move a foot a little to keep her balance. The concrete opened; the depths widened, but as it enveloped her, she was not lifted; she did not fall into it. The ground beneath her hardened, and her feet were part of it and held fast to it. She became solid, immovable. The tendrils of the pull reached over her shoulders, around her torso, but their fingers slipped and flailed and finally dropped away, unable to grasp her. Her head cleared and the land pulled her back.

* * *

Hussein had eased himself into the shadows of the olive tree again and was watching the people as they walked through the grove, gathering before the ritual. Conversations ended, voices drifted off, and the grove emptied of words. Hussein spent the slow minutes looking at the facial expressions, body language, anything that could betray whatever thoughts were in their minds. No one would speak during the ritual, and the silence afterward as people left was accompanied only by the music of the wind. He wanted to see something, what it was within them that brought them here, day after day. There were flitting traces, a quavering lip, a teary eye, but the faces, rather than taking on the rigidity of stifled emotion, relaxed. There was peace in them. The jaws were without tension, the lips were not pursed; the eyes were wide to the day, not focused on something in another place, another time. They were not trying to relive something gone; they were living something present. It was here around him, and he knew it was here, but it kept slipping away.

He was outside. The sun had just gone lower in the sky, and the shadows were growing longer against the light. Hussein backed against the trunk of the olive tree and closed his eyes. He breathed in. The scratch of shod feet in the sand repeated in his ears as the shapes passed him. It was a march, a cadence, and with it he let his body sink against the tree, letting it support him, give him its strength. The day was hot, and the shade was a comfort, even if the sense of being cooler, he knew, was mostly a trick of his mind.

The shouting jarred Hussein back into the moment. It came from somewhere off to his left, behind the crest of the hill. Heads around him turned, and a few men started to run back through the olive grove. Then he heard a few quick pops, a sound he knew well. Someone had fired an AK-47. He glanced toward the wall, wondering if the men behind the darkened slits at the top of the turret had heard anything. There was no way of knowing yet. Only the arrival of a gunship would reveal that. But he was sure they couldn't see past the top of the hill.

Around him, more people were moving toward the sounds, walking fast, shifting to a jog, then into a run. The shots had stopped, but the voices had gotten louder. Feet thumped in an accelerating staccato; women's skirts crackled around their legs in the breeze. A moment later Hussein found himself running as well, half stumbling over the coarse ground. He dodged among the trees, parrying low-hanging branches. They scratched his arms; the little cuts began to bleed. The voices, louder with each moment, were coming in bursts, unintelligible except for their tone, which was belligerent, angry. He rounded the side of the hill, out of sight of the wall, and the terrain flattened to the edge of the grove and the narrow road beyond that connected the neighboring villages. There, in the middle of the road, a crowd was growing. As he ran down the slight incline, he had to check his speed to keep his balance. The shouting was more and more distinct, mixed angry voices, male and female. One woman's cry pierced through the others, "Let me go, damn you! Let me go!" Male voices retorted with "whore" and "bitch." Other sporadic, tentative voices rose, shouting, "Let her go!" "Get out of here!" As the crowd swelled, new voices joined in and the shouts grew louder, more committed, more insistent.

Hussein reached the crowd and tried to push through to see what was happening. He shouldered himself forward, but hands shoved him from behind and the side and he could only try to zigzag. He found himself pressed from all sides, forced to move with the crowd, and powerless to do anything but try to stay upright to avoid falling under feet that were all digging in to press closer. It was a living mass, writhing and constricting, surging and ebbing, the people in it rocking back, then pushing forward in unison.

As he lifted his heels to see better, the bodies shifted. He felt a sharp pain in his ankle, and fell hard to the ground. A knee hit his head, stunning him for a second. He tried to roll to all fours to avoid being trampled, but he was knocked over again, and the forms of two men collapsed on top of him. Hussein twisted to shake them off but he had no leverage, and their weight pressed on his lungs. One man rolled off to the side. The pressure lifted, and Hussein tried to take a breath. The dust was thick from the shuffling feet centimeters from his face, and he choked on it, coughing, rasping in his throat. In his ear someone yelled, "Get up! Get up!" Fingers dug into his upper arms from both sides and yanked him to his feet. For a moment he couldn't put weight on his ankle and he tripped, almost falling again. But the fingers held him up, and an arm came over his shoulder to steady him as he hopped a few steps in place, testing the ankle. The pain subsided enough for him to use both feet to stand. The arm pulled away. The "Thank you" that had formed in his mind remained unspoken; he had no idea whom to say it to.

The crowd surged again. This time he was able to stay upright, and he moved with it. More yells from all around him, one right in his ear. "Let her go!" Body odor mixed with the stale smell of the road's dust. His face felt gritty, and his mouth tasted dirt. An elbow hit him in the back; a forearm hit his head. The mass rocked again. This time the bodies in front of him shifted enough for him to glimpse Aisha.

Hussein squeezed forward until he was just behind the front row of the crowd and could see clearly. Aisha's arms were being held by two men in *kaffiyehs* wrapped to show only their eyes. Each had an assault rifle slung over his shoulder. A third man was standing directly in front of her. She was in a frenzy, clothes ripped, her hair loose and whipping around her head. She twisted and pulled, spitting for the men to get their hands off her. More cries of "Let her go" came from all around Hussein now. Opposite the crowd, beyond Aisha, stood a group of perhaps ten men. Most of their faces were also covered by *kaffiyehs*, and several were armed. Hussein thought he recognized one man, maybe another as well, but he wasn't sure. He would have to speak to Abu Ahmad.

The man in front of Aisha raised his weapon and shot a burst into the air. For a brief moment the crowd recoiled. Hussein was squeezed hard from all sides. He had to breath in short, hurried gulps. The hot air was becoming filled with dust kicked up by dozens of feet, and he coughed on it. Then the mass of bodies surged forward, and the man had to take a step back. He shot into the air again. This time the crowd didn't react at all, just kept moving toward him. He turned his head and yelled something to the armed men. As he took another step back, he tripped. His rifle fell to the ground and disappeared under the feet of the crowd. The man scrambled to get upright, tripped again, falling to one knee before he was able to get traction and sprint over to his compatriots. Hussein heard more bursts of gunfire go off but the crowd had momentum now. Hussein lost sight of Aisha and the gunmen. More gunshots, nearer, then just the noise of shouting.

He was part of it, indistinguishable from those around him, integral to it and to them. He found himself pushing, yelling, moving with it as it coiled and stretched, coiled and stretched. Their bodies were now a single body that moved right, left, changing direction, stalking, searching for an opening. The feet it rode on hit the ground faster and faster; their clatter smoothed into a building rhythm, and Hussein found himself running, toward what he couldn't see.

The pressure around him lessened, and Hussein found that the crowd was thinning, opening. He caught snatches of movement ahead through the widening spaces between people, and realized they all were running down the road, chasing the gunmen. He caught a glimpse of a couple of flapping *kaffiyehs* in the distance. Forms sprinted past him, and he moved off to the side of the road to get out of the way. A man sat propped against an olive tree holding his arm. Blood was seeping through his fingers as a woman ripped his shirtsleeve to create a bandage. Another man was limping in his direction. He was supported by a boy, barely a teenager by his looks, who was talking non-stop, encouraging, prodding, getting the man to move forward despite his pain. A few others looked shaken. A woman walked by alone, taking each step and holding it, as if she were testing the pains in her body to see if they meant real injury. Hussein looked around for Aisha and noticed a small group of people gathered in the middle of the road about fifty meters away. Aisha was talking to them. She was nodding and making a dismissive movement with one hand—as if what had just happened was nothing important. Then, abruptly, she turned and began walking. The others had to jog to catch up, then kept in step with her. She turned into the olive grove and began to mount the hill, heading back on the path to the wall. Hussein looked around. Where before he had only seen the backs of heads in the crowd, now he saw faces. They were coming toward him, past him, heading for the wall. So he too turned.

He crossed the road and entered the grove, taking a slightly different route from Aisha, one that would take him back to the tree, where he would watch in the shadows. His ankle had swollen and throbbed with each step, so he could only make his way gingerly over the uneven ground. Half way to the crest of the hill, he looked back. The people were streaming among the trees, all in the same direction as Aisha. Many were limping; some had an exuberant look on their faces. A look of triumph, victory.

Hussein found the tree and took his place in the shadows again. He watched the crowd that he had been a part of return to the grove. There was something sinuous now about the flow, something alive, an echo, perhaps, of whatever had awoken within the crowd on the road earlier. A pumping of blood, of energy. The line formed, the watchers settled. Hussein took a deep breath, and as he did so, he felt his shoulders drop, as if something was being emptied out of him, a tension, a worry. He wanted to come out from under the tree, to take his place among the men and women. He belonged with them. But no, caution must rule. Hussein settled back in the shadows. A man not far off to his left was shaking his arms; another stretched his back and straightened his shoulders. Nearby, a woman's torso inflated under her robes, then her mouth pursed, and she exhaled. Hussein thought he could hear the rush of the long, heavy breath leave her body. All through the crowd, little individual motions rippled, flexing and releasing, down to the line where fingers were already twitching around the first stone.

* * *

There he was. It had to be him. He had come to the tree, looked back and then gone under its branches. And he was still there. Just for a moment, before he had gone back under the olive branches, Zev had seen him. The shadow had a face, a form. Zev's excitement plummeted as fast as it had risen. Shit. The guy looked like a million other Arabs: short beard, tanned skin, neither short nor tall, neither fat nor thin. Great description. The generic terrorist. Nothing he could take to a superior and say, "Sir, I think I have something." Even Dani would laugh at him. "Ooh, a scary Arab. No gun, no bomb, just a guy with a beard who can't take the heat. And you want us to let you shoot him? Just like that? Maybe you forgot why you pulled turret duty in the first place." He could hear it, and he sighed. They wouldn't take him seriously enough to order a follow-up. They'd say he was hallucinating, couldn't take the heat. Maybe they would be right. He was just going nuts here. Making things up to entertain himself. Giving himself more of a purpose than checking out other nut cases through his scope, day in, day out.

"Anything new?"

Dani was behind him. Zev hadn't heard him come up. Better concentrate on business. Zev glanced to his left. Dani had his field glasses to his eyes and was panning slowly across the line of throwers as the girl began her nonsense yet again. He was faking it mostly; he was just as bored as Zev.

"No. Same old shit."

Same old faces, same old rocks, same old dirt, same old witch-bitch. The only new thing was the face of the guy who couldn't take the heat.

They watched as the ritual went on. Nothing happened

that hadn't happened every day since the damn thing began. The only difference was the heat. Being hot was the only thing that told him time had passed. Weeks and weeks of this. He raised his head from the rifle. People were walking back up the hill. Shit!

Zev swung his rifle to the tree and hunched back down. Where was the bastard? He dialed up the magnification. Nothing. The guy was gone. Zev dialed back and found a group of men not far from the tree, receding from his view. Beards, all of them. That guy could be him. Blue shirt, yeah, the guy had worn a blue shirt. Any others with blue shirts? Dammit, yes. Two. Beards? Their faces were turned away. Maybe. One, yes. One, no. Zev tracked both men as well as he could, but a minute later they were out of view.

"Fuck!"

"Huh? What's that about?" Dani lowered his field glasses and looked at Zev.

"Nothing. I need a break."

"Sure. Take ten. Get something to drink."

Five minutes later, Zev was back in the turret, scanning the tree where the guy sat. He wanted to shoot a couple of limbs off. Bring the guy out, expose him. Find out who the hell he was. He wiped some sweat out of his eyes. What a waste of time this shit was.

* * *

Khalid watched Hana bike away home to prepare dinner. He would stay another hour or so, then close up. His little hardware store was in Saris, a larger village than Qalunya, but only a couple of kilometers away. On a good day, he sometimes walked there and back. It had been his grandfather's store, then his father's. Khalid had grown up with the store, played in its aisles before he could walk, learned to stock its shelves before he could read. He felt a part of it, and it was a part of his family. Now, since his father had gone to live with Khalid's sister in Ramallah, Khalid ran it alone. No, not alone. Hana helped with the books, and Fadi came in now and again when there wasn't work in Ramallah. Abdullah, of course, had done his share when he was in school, but he had wanted more than this and now he was far away. Aisha had helped for years, too, but she had wanted to become a teacher, not a shopkeeper, and that's what she had done. But what the choice had now done to her, he wasn't sure. Maybe she needed to leave, too, for her own sake.

There was a jar of rusted screws and bolts on the counter. It had always been there. His grandfather had told him the story once, just once. After escaping with his life and little else, having taken shelter with his wife's family, Khalid's grandfather had begun to sell odds and ends he scavenged from destroyed army vehicles and dumps, anything that could be salvaged—nails, screws, nuts, engine parts, little necessities to rebuild with. And so the business had grown, to a point. Its trade was fairly constant now, had been for years. Something that could reasonably be counted on. Enough to support him, Hana and the children. People were always building or repairing something, and they came to him.

Through the special sale notices patterning the window, Khalid could see a few people walking in the street, little groups, chatting, all coming from the same direction—the wall. The ritual was over for the day and people were returning home. Of course, everyone in Qalunya and Saris knew Aisha was his daughter. At first there had been nods of sympathy; now there were nods of respect.

A customer came in, Binjamin, a Jew from Beit Surik, an old settlement, built in 1977, that was about five kilometers away. Khalid had known him for years. Binjamin himself was slightly older than Khalid, but he too had grown up in these hills. He had started coming to the store because it was convenient, long before the days of the Separation Barrier and Israeli-only highways. Now he came here out of habit, though he liked to joke with Khalid that his real motivation was to avoid paying the high prices "the Jews" charged in Jerusalem. Binjamin liked to linger and tell Khalid about his home-improvement projects and his garden. He wore the traditional *kipa,* and *tzitzit* fringes hung down at his waist. Khalid gathered that Binjamin was some sort of village elder in his settlement, but Binjamin never discussed that or anything else to do with Beit Surik. And he had told him why once: "Oh, there are so many more interesting things to talk about, things I never get the chance to talk about at home." Khalid took him at his word, but he suspected that the newer, aggressive settlers gave him trouble. Binjamin wasn't like them. They imposed themselves on the land; he was part of it. He belonged here. He was respectful, always asked after Khalid's children, a genial man, a funny man. And he was devout, a true man of the Book. He and Khalid had always been able to find a common interest or concern to chat about. Above all, Binjamin was a shuffler, a putterer. Always doing something. Always productive, as Binjamin himself liked to say. Khalid suspected that Binjamin acted older than he was because he imagined himself to be that way, older, a creature of his traditions. Wiser perhaps, than if he tried to act young all the time. A funny man.

Binjamin spent a few minutes looking over some new hand tools. He always did, but hadn't bought one in a long time. He took good care of his tools, Khalid had decided. In the end, Binjamin chose a box of finishing nails and a few packets of sandpaper and came to the counter.

"A little job in the kitchen."

Khalid scanned the purchases, and Binjamin paid. Khalid waited for the inevitable musing on whatever concerns had been rumbling around Binjamin's mind, the start of a back-and-forth that could easily fill the last hour of the work day. This would be welcome today, which had been rather quiet. But Binjamin just picked up the bag when Khalid was done and moved toward the door. He had his hand on the door handle when he turned and came back to the counter. He stopped when he was just beyond arm's length from Khalid.

"Those people out there."

He gestured to the people walking in the street.

"Yes."

"They're coming from the Separation Barrier, from the stone throwing, am I correct?"

A silence, a reluctance. Khalid waited.

"It's sad, yes, very sad. I heard what happened. Those poor children. What a waste."

Another silence. Binjamin stepped closer and leaned against the counter.

"I was told the girl there is your daughter. I feel sorry for her. Will she be all right? Doing this thing in the heat, it can't be good for her."

"She'll be all right."

Binjamin walked over to a table and picked up one of the flashlights lying there. There was a special on LED flashlights this week. He flicked the light on and off and pointed it down the aisle, now getting dark in the late afternoon. The LED gave off a bluish light, rather than the yellow light of incandescent light bulbs. Colder, but the LED lasted longer.

"Why does she do this? Every day, isn't it? It seems, and

I'm sorry to say this, more than a bit crazy."

Binjamin was surprised when Khalid gave a short laugh. "It does, doesn't it?"

"Is she all right? In the head I mean."

"I think so. It's just something she says she has to do."

Binjamin took this in and nodded.

"I think I understand. It makes me feel sad, all that stone throwing. I don't like sadness. We live with it too much. It would be nice not to have so much."

Binjamin was shaking his head. It was theatrical, Khalid thought, but in the way a moment on stage concentrates a gesture that might otherwise be mundane.

"Why does she do it? Every day. All that time."

Khalid shrugged. He thought it best not to say anything.

"You know, that wall there, it's not going to move. And yet they all go there. Those people with their pebbles. What do they expect? We only have so much time. Why spend it on futility? Better to plant a tree, dig a ditch."

Binjamin's voice got lower, closer.

Khalid wouldn't have said Binjamin was a friend exactly—a customer, a good acquaintance, close to a friend, but there were distances between them. But now, Binjamin was his friend, he had no doubt; at least for this moment, man to man, he saw a friend in front of him.

"Maybe all they can do is this. Maybe they're lost. All I can think is that they are lost. Lost in their grief. Like in the desert. Hopeless. I feel so sad for them. Does that make sense?"

The lines at the corners of Binjamin's mouth softened and melted into his cheeks. His whole face became slack. Still. He shrugged, reached over the counter, and grasped Khalid's forearm. The pressure of Binjamin's fingers was strong, and then was urgent.

"Don't lose your child. Don't lose her."

A quick, nearly painful squeeze and the hand slipped away. Binjamin picked up his purchases again and this time walked out the door. He got into a small car, but didn't pull out immediately. Khalid could see him sitting in the driver's seat, watching the last stragglers from the ritual walk by. Only when the streets were clear did the engine start and the car back out and turn into the road north toward Beit Surik.

Khalid got a broom and began to sweep the floor as he did every day. He heard the door open and looked up.

"That Jew. Abu Abdul, you know him?"

The man in the doorway was Hamza, a local man. Khalid knew him slightly.

"Yes. He's a customer."

"I think I saw him yesterday."

"He comes to the village often. Says it's cheaper here."

"No. I mean at the wall, at the ritual."

"Really. He didn't tell me."

"He stood to the side, all by himself. You couldn't miss him, after all, an old man with his beard and his *kipa*, those tassels hanging down at his belt. He wasn't doing anything, just watching, so we ignored him."

"He was there the whole time?"

"Oh, yes. Longer actually."

"Longer?"

"I looked back. Some friends and I were talking right where the path goes around the hill and I could see him. He was walking down the hill toward the wall. So I watched him. I mean, what the hell is a Jew even doing there? Anyway, I kept watching. He goes right up to the wall and touches it, keeps his hand on it for a long time. Then he turned around. I didn't want him to notice me so I left. Strange. What do you think he was doing?"

Khalid thought of the old Jew, then of the Jew who acted old, and he remembered the day a few years ago when he had asked Binjamin why his hair was so long. The old man was usually so meticulous in his appearance. It had taken a long time for him to speak. "I'm sitting shiva," was what Binjamin had finally said.

"He had a little boy who died. Maybe that's why."

Hamza looked about to say something, but stopped. After a few seconds, he gave a short nod, not to Khalid, but as if he were punctuating a thought. Then he said good-bye and left.

Binjamin hadn't told Khalid that day; it only came out later. Binjamin came in a couple of weeks later for some small thing. His hair was still uncut, and he looked more like a sad, lonely dog than anything else. One day the kid was running after friends, like any boy anywhere. The next day a pain in his leg sent him to the hospital. A tumor. Inoperable. Random.

"You lose them, you know. All of them. It's just a matter of how."

Khalid had nodded, and Binjamin saw that Khalid understood what he had meant. Binjamin was stuck in the rhythms of aging, caught up in routines that were supposed to give comfort, some insulation from what the passage of time can do. Khalid supposed this was happening to him. He hoped not. He had lost Abdul to the outside world; he hoped this wasn't forever. Was he losing Fadi, too? And to what? Even a child's adulthood is a loss to the parents. Fadi was at that stage, an adult in age and a growing awareness of it. Would he leave, too, when time wrapped him in its folds? And Aisha, where was she? Here and not here. Present and not present. She was rocking back and forth on the edge of a divide. Would she fall over that edge? Or was she already gone?

Khalid decided not to sweep the floor. He needed to get outside. He would leave his bicycle here and walk home, let himself be distracted by shadows, by birds flitting noisily in the trees, by the sway of dry grass in the wind, by what every afternoon offered when he took the time to pay attention.

Chapter 10

The watchers were dispersing on the other side of the grove, Hussein among them. By now, he could almost exactly pace off the distance between the olive tree where he watched and the corner of the nearest building, where he would turn and disappear into the village. It was an exposed route in part, but shielded enough from the turret so he could walk freely. He was careful to look away as much as he could, leaving only, he hoped, a vague, indecipherable profile. He had had practice, much practice. His eyes tracked the ground and his thoughts were centered on blending in with the others leaving the ritual, his form one of many. A laborer, perhaps, a truck driver, an ordinary man. Nothing to distinguish him.

"Brother Hussein!"

Hussein turned just enough to identify the speaker out of the corner of his eye. It was Abdullah al-Zahir, about ten

183

meters away, slightly lower on the hill, and Hussein had a clear line of sight to the observation tower behind him. Abdullah raised his hand in a gesture of greeting. Hussein pivoted sharply back around and made sure he was not walking any faster than before. The man he had been walking next to had moved away; Hussein stepped to the right, just behind a heavy-set woman who gave him a cautious look out of the corner of her eye. He let a small gap grow between them, and her glance moved away.

"Brother Hussein!"

The voice was now at his side, panting from a sprint to catch up. Hussein did not look at him.

"Walk with me, Abdullah."

The sound of Abdullah's footfalls became stumbling echoes of Hussein's as Abdullah tried to match strides with him.

"You should know better than to do that."

It was clear what Hussein meant.

"I'm sorry, but I wanted to catch you. Abu Ahmad wants to see you. He's just up ahead."

They reached the corner and went right, into a narrow street whose shadows were already deep in the late afternoon. They found Abu Ahmad fifty meters farther on, standing in a doorway, barely visible. He stepped forward as Hussein came up to him.

"Do you have time to talk?"

Hussein nodded. A few streets later they found a small convenience store and went in. Abdullah bought bottles of water for each of them, and they went to stand against the wall at the back where they could see whoever came in.

"Have you talked to the girl?"

Hussein looked down the street. A woman was crossing the next intersection, pulling a child along by its hand. Abu Ahmad waited. Hussein took a breath and sighed.

"She's difficult."

"How do you mean?"

How could he describe the girl? The image of her face rose in his mind, her eyes fixed on him and her mouth ranting, cursing, berating. She hadn't listened to anything he had said. She was stubborn, argumentative, and rude. And blasphemous. Oh, yes. Rude and blasphemous described her well.

"It was hard to get through to her. She was very angry. Is angry."

"She was disrespectful?"

"You might say."

Disrespectful was about the kindest word for her. Hussein realized he felt amused by that, and this disoriented him for a moment.

"You offered our assistance if she behaved more appropriately?"

"I tried to."

"She didn't listen?"

"No, she just said a few things, then left the room. It wasn't a real discussion. Her parents apologized. They were quite embarrassed."

"As well they might be."

Abu Ahmad's forehead wrinkled.

"Did she show any sense of propriety at all?"

Hussein's mouth twitched with a thin smile.

"Barely any."

Abu Ahmad turned and took a sip of water before looking back at Hussein.

"I'm very concerned about this. Abdullah tells me more and more people come every day to this display she puts on. At some point it will get out of hand. I'm coming to the opinion that perhaps we should take measures to end this, put her in her place. The best for all concerned. Even her."

Hussein shook his head, again looking at the ground.

"I've been watching this performance, this ritual, for several weeks now. Not every day, but often, and I'm not sure it wouldn't be best just to let things run their course."

"But she's an affront to everything we stand for!"

A look from Abu Ahmad reminded Abdullah that respect was owed.

"She's an insult"—the tone was now measured—"and that makes what she is doing dangerous."

Abdullah's lips pursed with conviction.

Hussein saw the eagerness, the need, in the younger man; his passions practically screamed for company. But

186

Hussein could not join him. Time had taken away the fire, the heat, and now his actions were ruled by the cold reason of his mind. He could only be alone. This is what the years do to us, to some of us, he thought. He felt a momentary pull of empathy for Abdullah, for his youth. And sadness that only time would be able to do what he, the elder, could not.

Hussein took a heavy breath.

"I do not see that. Not yet."

Abu Ahmad looked over Hussein's face carefully. Neither spoke. The tips of Hussein's fingers twisted the cap of his water bottle with no hurry—up and down, up and down, up and down. He knew Abu Ahmad was watching his expression, looking for a signal, a sign of agreement, of shared commitment. A common bond in the struggle. But the years had taught him to submerge his private thoughts to such depths that nothing broke through to his expression unless bidden. Now, though, even he didn't know what he thought, so the blankness was real on both sides.

Abu Ahmad's stare softened into a reflection of the calm of his own. Abdullah began to fidget, and Hussein knew it was time to speak.

"It will end. It is not sustainable, this fruitlessness. If nothing else, the heat of the summer will push people away. And we should just let it happen. We might look very bad if we tried to interfere. I think that all we would do is embarrass ourselves. We would come across as afraid of her, and we need not be."

187

Abdullah stiffened.

"What? Of course we're not afraid of her. She is nothing."

"Then perhaps we would be wasting our time to interfere."

Another silence. Hussein watched the proprietor sell a newspaper to a man and chat with him amiably.

"She misleads people. She does not know her place. She behaves like—what can I say?—a woman who has no morals, no sense of values, of decency. And yet people join her in this pitiful exercise!"

Abdullah's voice had risen. He paused.

"We cannot be seen to tolerate this." The tone was now quieter, but still strained with urgency. "This dishonors our struggle. We look like fools, like trembling old men with no spines. To let a girl take our place. We must force her to obey, to honor the struggle properly, not with little rocks thrown by women and old men, but with resistance."

Abdullah looked at Hussein again, intently trying to find something in his face. He didn't find anything and looked away.

"What she is doing, it is against the struggle. That's why it must be stopped."

Again, no ripple on his face revealed what was churning in Hussein's mind.

"The struggle is about fighting those who are against us. It's about resistance. Real resistance. It is about strength. She is teaching passivity, surrender. What is she doing to the enemy? Is she hurting them? Is she making them pay for what they have done to us, what they do to us every day? The Zionists are laughing at her and at us. Only strength, only force, only solidarity will get them to take us seriously, to give back what they have stolen. Our land, our dignity."

Hussein had heard this before. He had said it before. He had nothing to say now. The proprietor had been glancing over at them every now and then. Now he was beginning to stare. It was time to go.

"The people need leadership. Our leadership. I know I am young. I look to you—I am asking you, stop this girl, this filthy exhibitionist, before she harms our cause."

"Her struggle is less important than ours. Is that what you are saying?"

"Of course. What use is it? What can she accomplish? She is leading our people into emptiness."

"You are impatient."

"Of course I am. We have waited long enough. It is time to act, again and again, until our struggle is finished and we have won."

Hussein shook his head.

"The struggle is never over. This is what I have learned."

Abdullah looked at Hussein, searching his face again.

"You have lost hope. You are broken. The struggle has been too much for you."

"Perhaps it has. But let me suggest something. We do not know what will happen with this girl. I will try again to gain her confidence. At the very least I will watch to see that no one else tries to control her or what she is doing."

Abu Ahmad stood for a few moments, then straightened.

"All right. For now, Hussein, we will wait." He raised a hand for Abdullah to be silent. "Let us hope that this is the correct course. And now we should leave. It is almost time for prayers."

* * *

Mumtaz was silent as always, but Hussein could feel his driver's disapproval. He was going to walk on the streets in the open again. But there was nothing he could do to stop himself. He had to think, and the car on this hot day was just too confining, too stifling. He shrugged as Mumtaz pulled away and turned into a dark silhouette in the driver's seat. Hussein began to walk. He stuck his hands in his pockets for a few seconds, then pulled them out again and shook each of them in the air, as if something was on them that he had to get off. But there wasn't. He kicked at a stone. A piece of used newspaper was lying in front of him. He wanted to pick it up, neaten the path, but he stopped himself. What was he doing? This aimlessness, this fidgeting?

He had taken a risk. He didn't like it, but he had done it anyway. Abu Ahmad had accepted his choice—reluctantly;

he didn't like to create conflict, not at their level. Perhaps, Hussein had counted on that. Once Abu Ahmad assented, Abdullah hadn't dared object too strongly. Nor would anyone else. Perhaps he had counted on that as well.

He knew what they thought of him. The planner, the plotter. What did he always say to them, these zealots, these warriors with the flames of glory in their eyes? "Reduce your risk to as close to zero as possible." To the soldiers of the faith, he was cold, distant. Airless. Someone who sucked the fire out of their cause. Where was his spark, his passion for the struggle?

He did not know. His feet were planted on the ground—in reality. It was his mind, his cold reason that kept his heart beating. He did not lead with his heart. Not any more. Survival was not a risk-taking activity; it was a risk-reduction activity. He had survived. And he tried not to spend time thinking of those impassioned soldiers who hadn't.

He knew many of the others feared him, too. He didn't discourage it. Fear was useful. He found trust ephemeral. You tried to stand on it—to rely on its firmness, its constancy—and it vanished. One of his first hard lessons in the struggle. Fear gels nicely into something of substance.

Fear is easy, too. You can take the slightest ember of it and stoke it until its heat is all anyone feels. He used to enjoy that, playing with the zealots to get them in line. Make them productive. But it had become a tired game—a chore. With time he had left the incessant disciplining to others, and retreated with his disappointment into the ranks of authority.

Now age had made him venerable, too. Because he was a survivor, his life was veneered with respect. But the apprehension was there still. Few knew what he did. Or what he had done. And he had done things, necessary things, but he was relieved to have left them behind—for others whose blood ran hotter than his. Blood likes blood. He didn't like blood. He hadn't for a long time. He stopped and looked down at the sidewalk. Then he looked at the road. Flat surfaces. Pristine when new, even, smooth. That was long ago. What he was looking at was not new. There were cracks and grooves. Quick scars, slow erosion, constant abrasion. A mirror of life.

The girl—the risk. Why did he take it? Why did he put himself in this position of—what? Guard dog? Nursery maid? Spy? Hussein searched in his mind for a reason, an explanation. There was none. He had just done it. An impulse, a whim. No, that was not right. Whims are trivial, selfish. He had no self anymore. He had only a need. He didn't understand it, but he accepted it as true, as right. He knew it was right. She had to be left alone, kept insulated from people like Abdullah. It was a role he had to play, therefore a risk he had to take. And was it a risk at all? Maybe to others—maybe to himself, a few moments ago. But now it wasn't. It wasn't a risk at all. It was an acceptance —an acceptance of what needed to be.

He looked down the street ahead of him. A few meters farther, a flowerpot stood beside a door. A speck of green leaves and red blooms nurtured through the dryness and heat. He had no idea what sort of flower it was. A common flower, something people usually took for granted. But now, it was summer. Water was precious and someone was giving it to this—a plant, an existence completely dependent on charity, whose only function was to break monotony with a little color that some called beauty. He didn't know what he called it.

He realized he had stopped walking. He had been staring —at the pavement, at the flower. He didn't know for how long. He shook his head to pierce the bubble of stopped time that had enclosed him. His feet began moving by themselves, a quick stride—too urgent, he thought. They slowed to a comfortable pace, and he let them carry him down the street. As he passed it, he allowed himself a glance at the flower, then turned his attention forward and took command of his direction, lest his feet take him somewhere he was sure he didn't want to go.

* * *

"Aisha is in over her head, Father. You know this."

Khalid grunted. Fadi was unsure whether this meant agreement or just recognition of what Fadi had said.

"Women shouldn't do such things. It isn't right."

193

Khalid turned to his son. Fadi was his youngest and most volatile in temperament, at least until recently. Fadi's sister seemed to be making up for a quiet youth.

"Why do you say that?"

"It's part of our faith, part of what our people are."

"No it isn't, Fadi. You should be more careful about what you say regarding our faith.

"But it's what we are taught."

"I'm sure it is, but that doesn't mean it's correct."

"But men should lead men. Women shouldn't lead men. Aisha should stay home, get married or something."

"She embarrasses you, doesn't she?"

Fadi stiffened.

"No, that's not it!"

"I think it is. Look, a lot of what we are taught is tradition. That's fine, we need to appreciate our traditions, but we shouldn't pretend we live a thousand years ago."

"But some things are always true, no matter what century we are in."

"I agree. But what things?"

"Well, like obedience to God."

"Yes, obedience to God, not necessarily obedience to men."

"But we need men to lead us."

"We need people to lead us. Whether they are men or women is, I think, irrelevant."

"But it is our role in life! We are the heads of our families, not women."

"You might change that opinion once you get married."

"How do you mean?"

"Marriage, like so many things, is a partnership. We just each have our separate roles. Neither husband nor wife is inherently superior. Not in marriage and not before God. It's the same in life. We men cannot pretend we are superior to women. It is arrogant, immodest. Blasphemous really. True faith requires that we be modest, humble before life and God."

"But you let Aisha go out that way! Making a display of herself every day!"

"You think she is immodest?"

"Of course."

"Does she flirt, wear revealing clothes, behave inappropriately toward anyone?"

"What do you call her stone-throwing, then if not immodest?"

"Well, I was very worried at first. Not about immodesty, more about how she didn't care how she looked or acted. Your mother and I talked about it a lot. As a team." Khalid looked sternly at his son. "Yes, as a team. Aisha is the daughter of both of us, not just me. Then I went to see what she was doing. I went several times. And I saw as she calmed down, too. Day by day she became less wild, more serious, even respectful."

"Respectful? Of what?"

"Of what she was doing."

"I don't get what you mean. She's throwing rocks at the wall. It's pointless."

"It isn't pointless, just different. Your sister has been through a lot. She hasn't been well. Maybe she needs this. Maybe those other people throwing rocks with her all need to do it, too, just because. And who are we to judge? Who is anyone to judge?"

Fadi wanted to say something but found he had no words.

"Are you staying for dinner?"

"Yes, I think so."

"Good, come with me."

Khalid led his son out of the house and toward the wall.

"You want me to watch Aisha?"

"I think you need to—as her brother."

Fadi shrugged. He would humor his father.

* * *

They were early and sat under an olive tree to wait. After a while, people started to arrive. First individuals appeared, then long single-file lines formed, snaking down the hill. The throwers continued to the bottom; everyone else found a spot to wait on the slope of the hill. Khalid and Fadi saw Aisha come down the hill in measured steps. She spoke to no one, and no one tried to speak to her. She took her place in front of the wall, and Fadi became aware of the silence—not an empty silence, an absence, but a full silence, a presence. The silence surrounded them and Fadi felt somehow sheltered by it, even though there was nothing but sky above his head.

The ritual began. The arcs of the stones were nearly identical. Instead of flying as insignificant bits of rock, they took on depth together, like a long wave breaking on the shore. Fadi had seen the sea once, long ago when he was a child and travel was easier. They had wanted to go to the beach, but a storm had risen and all they could do was watch. He remembered the water and its power, whipped by the wind. He had been afraid and his father had held him and told him it would be all right tomorrow. And it had been.

The calling of the names surprised him today. He had come once before and had barely noticed the names. Now he did, and saw the mouths of the throwers move. It was a chant, melodious in its way. After the twelfth stone, the sound drifted away, but he could still hear it in his mind as the last throw, the thirteenth, echoed alone. With that, Aisha began to leave and the crowd watched her go. The silence seemed to dissipate, and they were out in the open again.

* * *

Hussein's cell phone rang later that evening. When he finally hung up he nearly cursed out loud.

But of course, it was inevitable. A demonstration near the Qalandya crossing point had erupted a few hours before. It had followed much the same pattern as Aisha's ritual—throwing rocks at the separation barrier and shouting a name for each one—except that the names they yelled were martyrs to the cause, who had died with blood on their hands. When the rocks were done, however, there had been a barrage of AK-47 fire at the wall as a coda. Israeli soldiers had rushed to the scene and exchanged fire with the protesters. Seven had been arrested, some of whom were wounded. The caller didn't know if any Israelis had been hit.

Hussein tried to calm down. He saw what it was, a copycat protest, an escalation, taking someone else's idea and expropriating it. This group simply tweaked the formula, made it louder, brasher, more attention-getting. It would be on the news in Israel tonight. That, naturally, was the point.

He wondered if Abdullah had anything to do with it. The girl wasn't jihadi enough for him. Abdullah wanted a Quranic veneer that she wasn't providing. He wasn't wrong in this, just too emotional, too impatient. If what they did was not rooted in scripture, what was it worth? If your blood is shed as a martyr, you are holy. If not, you are just dead. This was the struggle they never talked about, the struggle to keep to the path and not be tempted away. And the temptations were many. This last protest was clumsy, hurried, poorly conceived, doomed to become a caricature. Impatient, he thought, so they send off idiots drugged on the catharsis of violence. "To make idiots of all of us," he added, speaking to no one.

Chapter 11

There was a crash of breaking wood and yelling in the front of the house. The bedroom door burst open. Khalid and Hana were blinded by lights attached to gun barrels.

"Out of bed!"

Dark forms moved behind the light—soldiers. Rough hands took handfuls of cloth near their necks, and Hana and Khalid were pushed and dragged into the living room.

"On the floor! Kneel! Hands behind your heads!"

"What's happening?"

"Shut up! On your knees. Hands on your heads!"

They did as they were told. Moments later, Fadi was shoved down beside them. He tried to stand.

"Down, you."

"Fuck you!"

"Fadi! Do as they say!"

"What do they want? Aisha! Aisha, where are you?"

Voices came from Aisha's room.

"You, girl. Stand up."

Aisha was led out by two dark forms and thrown to the ground. One form took out a small, rectangular shape—a photograph—and held it at arm's length.

"It's her. You! Get dressed."

"Aisha, what's happening?"

"Shut up!" shouted a voice above them.

"Get dressed, I said!"

"In front of you?"

"I've seen women naked before. You're not so special."

A flashlight was trained on Aisha. A bunch of clothes was dropped in front of her, the ones she had worn yesterday and left on a chair in her room.

"Here. Move!"

Aisha pulled a loose robe over her shoulders and tried to dress as much as possible under its cover.

"Hurry up!"

Aisha finished pulling up a long skirt, and found a shawl to put over her shoulders.

"I'm ready."

A hand grabbed her arm.

"Let's go."

She just had time to look back at her parents and brother kneeling on the floor, two soldiers standing behind them, the muzzles of their TAR 21s within inches of their heads, before she was shoved into the rear of an armored vehicle.

Hana looked up at the soldier standing over her.

"Where are you taking her?"

There was no response. A call came from the street.

"She's in!"

"Right! Withdraw!"

The soldiers guarding Khalid, Hana, and Fadi now backed out the door, weapons still trained on the kneeling figures. Three armored vehicles stood outside the house, their motors running. The soldiers got into the last one. They all sped off toward the Beitunya crossing.

* * *

Khalid, his wife, and son sat on the couch without speaking. Khalid had his arm around Hana. Fadi didn't want to be touched.

"Give me a second. I need to call the Civil Police."

Khalid stood up and took out his cell phone.

"What good will that do? No one can do anything."

"Fadi, we still have to report it. Maybe they can find out where she has been taken."

Fadi stood up and paced in front of his mother while Khalid had a brief conversation with the nighttime police operator. Hana sat on the couch with her arms crossed, grasping her body as if she were having difficulty keeping warm.

"They'll send a car in the morning. They told us all to try to get some sleep."

"Ha!" Fadi slammed the door to his room. Khalid sat down next to Hana and wrapped both arms around her. They were still there, awake, at dawn.

* * *

At the wall that afternoon, there was confusion, doubt. The murmuring of the crowd was audible in the sniper's nest. The throwers had spread out but had not formed a line. They stood uneasily and did not step toward the wall. The men in the turret were on edge. The word had come down that morning that the witch had been arrested.

"Dani?" Zev spoke without taking his eye off his scope. "Do you think we should try to disperse them?"

"No orders to. Let's see what happens."

Still the throwers did not move. A few clenched and unclenched their fists around the rocks they held, but most just stood there, waiting. Voices rose and died. After a while, no one spoke anymore and silence began to fill the empty space that Aisha's absence had created. Even the wind seemed to die down. People stopped shuffling their feet and stood still, a long human hedge opposite the looming concrete in front of them. Several minutes passed. People cast their eyes downward, lost, thoughtful maybe. Even through his scope, it was hard for Zev to tell. Their expressions betrayed little.

One man finally lifted his head and stepped forward. Zev focused his scope on him. Zev remembered the face. The man was one of the first who had joined the girl, a gaunt man, looking more tired and worn than a man should be, even here. Zev had no name for him. The man took a stone from his pocket and held it up, but instead of throwing it, he waited. Another man a few feet away stepped forward and then, smoothly, everyone who had been hesitating did, and the line formed. Each took out a stone and held it high. They all waited until everyone up and down the line had done the same. And the ritual began.

"Nassim!" came out of the hundred or so voices. Zev panned the crowd, focusing on the faces, on the leaders. The wind picked up and carried the name up to and over the wall, and, as its echo died, the stones followed rhythmically. The chorus of names then rose from the crowd as they had for the past weeks, the clatter of stones punctuating each. Virtually in unison, their voices louder than usual, possessed of a new edge of anger and determination, the crowd performed as by rote. The soldiers in the turret looked, sensing something building, flexing within the bodies before them. Their hands tightened for assurance around the stocks of their weapons.

Zev watched. The crowd yelled "Ali!" and he saw the face of the first man who had stepped forward tighten as a memory of pain flickered across it. Zev knew the look. He had seen it on his aunt's face when they had buried his cousin after he was killed in the war in Lebanon. She had died the next year. And only after she died had the expression left her.

As the last stones clattered against the wall, a silence fell over the crowd again, and they still stood, making no motion to leave, as if something had not yet released them from its hold. Long moments passed. Some of their expressions began to look a bit lost again. Then a single, young voice rang out. "Aisha!" This unexpected interruption sparked a staggered response, with cries of "Aisha" bursting forth here and there up and down the line of people paralleling the wall. There was movement—bodies arching, arms waving, fists shaking—but no one broke ranks. Gathering unity and force, the name rippled through the crowd into the distance, a giant wave breaking on the concrete with each utterance. The first, small voice shouted out again and again, seven times in all, waiting each time as the sound of Aisha's name receded into the distance before shouting it again. Then he stopped, and they all stood again in silence.

Zev scanned what faces he could. He saw the tiredness, the drained expressions after the effort. But he didn't see what he thought he would. He saw no anger. No venting frustration. No resignation in defeat. He wasn't sure exactly, but he thought what he saw was elation, purpose. It made no sense to him. In any case, the long chain of people along the wall was now slowly breaking apart, each person moving back toward home, some alone, some in groups. Not a lot of talk, it seemed to him, but at least they were leaving.

Zev watched them go, and as he did, a sensation overcame him. It was discomfiting, a mixture of respect and shame, and his back and neck felt crusted with a kind of cold tightness he couldn't place. He didn't like feeling this; he didn't like feeling anything, really, as far as Arabs were concerned. How long had it been drilled into him? These people were unclean, like so many barnyard swine, not fit for human company, not fit to live on holy land—not worth a moment's thought or emotion that one might have for a real human being.

Arabs were targets, not people. They were a threat. What had been drummed into him during basic training? "Fear is your friend. It keeps you alive." What they meant wasn't fear, though. They meant: "Don't trust your enemy at all, except for one thing—trust him to always try to kill you." He had never feared and never trusted. He watched his front and his back. And he never missed. That's why he was alive and his targets weren't.

The unwelcome sensation hurt more now, a caustic churning in his gut and chest. He tried to ignore it and continued to survey the crowd as it dispersed. He caught sight of the first man, the thin one who had taken over for the witch. He was walking alone just on the other side of the road and was about to start climbing the hill. Another man came up to him and touched him on the arm. There was a shared nod, and the two parted. The thin man moved up a narrow path between the trees. His steps were slow, a bit labored. His head was bent, watching the ground. It took forever for him to get to the top of the hill.

"Dani, do you mind if I take a break?"

"Sure, take fifteen. Aaron will take over for a while."

Zev stood up and walked down the circular stairs in the tower to the medium-sized space one floor below that served as break room and locker room. There he laid his rifle on a table; it looked filthy to him. He walked over to his locker and searched in it for a small kit bag. Finding it, he sat down at the table. He applied gun oil to a cloth and began to clean the weapon, inside and out, rubbing as hard as he could to get the grime out of the barrel and breech mechanism. The fine dirt seemed to be oozing from the steel. He wiped it again and again but there was always residue on the cloth. Dani's voice broke his concentration. His superior was standing right in front of him, his hands on his hips.

"Zev, what the hell are you doing? I said fifteen, not fifty. Get topside, now!"

Zev looked up with a start. He tried to find his bearings for a second.

"Yes, Dani, sir!"

Dani looked at him.

"You all right?"

"Yeah, sure. Just needed a break."

Dani nodded and left, his steps echoing on the metal stairs as he ascended to the turret. Zev looked at his rifle. It was clean, very clean, he had to admit. But there were still traces of dust on it.

"Fuck it."

He gathered his stuff together and followed Dani.

* * *

"A girl? A schoolteacher? Are you kidding?" Colonel Andrei Beletsky shook his head. "Haven't we better things to do than interrogate a God-damned schoolteacher?"

He looked over at Joshua Greenberg, his subordinate in rank, but in Andrei's mind, an equal part of his team. And they both took orders from above. They had thirty-two suspects in the attack on the Qalandya checkpoint, all hardened terrorists by the look of them. And the brass wanted them to bust this girl, who looked as if she were half nuts.

Joshua was shaking his head.

"Two things. One, this so-called girl is a leader of some weird protest or something. She's an instigator, and what she's doing is clearly tied to what happened at Qalandya somehow. The similarities are too striking. Maybe it was her idea. We have to find out. Two, if we move now, we control, to the extent possible, any sort of reaction. We can move in, clean up, establish necessary rules and curfews, and smash this thing before Hamas, Fatah, or someone else starts to manipulate it for their own ends. That is, if they haven't

208

already done so."

There was no response to that. Their relationship was contentious at times, which suited Andrei. The two of them would tire each other out with long debates, before Andrei asserted his rank and made his decision. Andrei had seen enough to know he wasn't perfect, and, even if Joshua was too eager, too aggressive, Andrei knew he needed to hear him out. He had to hear the other side to feel he was right.

"Okay." Andrei had made his decision. "Let's find out what she knows."

* * *

Ever since they had removed her blindfold and shoved her into the cell, she had been in the dark. She had no idea how long. Hours maybe. It was cold, too, as if the air conditioning was turned on high, and maybe it was. Her skin, her bones wracked with shivers. Her summer clothes were too light for this. She wrapped the shawl around her as tightly as she could, but it was thin and offered little warmth.

She had fallen into the faceless void again and was floating, directionless. The warmth was seeping out of her, its absence pooling, congealing around her feet until they were numb. There were no sounds, either. No footsteps from the corridor, which had to be close but may as well have been in another dimension. If she made a sound, if she spoke, it was muffled, as if it had never escaped her, as if it had never been uttered. This is what a tomb is like, she thought. She had no idea how big the cell was. It felt enormous and tiny at the same time. She hugged herself for warmth and closed her eyes because there was no point in keeping them open. She began to fall, down into the maw of infinity.

A heavy click and light poured through her eyelids, jarring her awake. Soon, in another, warmer room, she was told to sit in a chair, and the interrogation began. Her life was set out before her. She was told to remember, to remember everything. There were two, and they alternated. She never knew which would speak next. They asked different questions, then the same question, but in different ways. They were attentive when she answered, as if each word out of her mouth was important. Did you know about the demonstration at Qalandya? No. Why not? Weren't you told? No. Who do you report to? No one. Are you a terrorist? No. Is anyone in your family a terrorist? No. Do you know any terrorists? No. Why do you throw those stones? I don't know. What are you trying to accomplish? I don't know. Why do you keep doing it? I don't know. When will you stop? I don't know. Do you want revenge? No. Why not? I don't know. Do you believe in God? I don't know. Why not? I don't know.

Hours passed. They would take irregular breaks when they would leave the room. Time would pass. Then the door would slam open, and they were there again. Once they gave her something to eat. More questions. For how long she couldn't tell. When they were done, she was told to stand up and was led to another cell where there was a cot with a thin blanket. They left her there without turning off the light. There was no switch. She lay down and pulled the blanket over her. The room was cold, like the first one, and she pulled herself into a ball to try to get warm.

Time lost its meaning. If she slept, she was shaken awake and pulled out to be questioned again. The rooms were warm, cold, light, dark. Her interrogators were friendly; they were belligerent. They spoke for hours or minutes. She ate; she went hungry. She slept; she was dragged awake.

She was spinning round—spinning webs, tales, wool to make her warm. Everything spun around her, sparks of light shooting off, flashing on the buttons of coats hung on chairs, augering her down into unconsciousness.

* * *

Aisha's release came about as suddenly as her arrest. At 6 a.m., three days after she was taken, a sand-colored IDF Zeev 2 armored vehicle stopped at the Qalandya checkpoint. A soldier got out and walked into a low concrete building next to the road. The checkpoint consisted of a series of passageways with a gate on each end. The walls of the passageways were rows of spaced steel rods. Corrugated fiberglass formed a peaked roof overhead. At the end of each passageway was a guard station with a group of armed soldiers. One soldier checked papers, while the others searched bags and belongings. Already the line of Palestinian civilians waiting to cross was long, snaking back to a parking lot on the other side of the separation barrier. Guards and civilians alike watched obliquely as the soldier came back out of the building and got into the Zeev 2.

"They won't let us leave her here. They don't want another riot."

The three others swore. The driver looked at him.

"Well, what the hell are we supposed to do with her, take her home like we're some goddamn taxi?"

"They said there's a bus stop a couple of kilometers up the road. We should dump her there."

The driver nodded and put the vehicle into gear. A few minutes later, it stopped next to a covered bus shelter standing under a group of trees. The rear doors opened, and a soldier got out. He scanned the area with a few jerks of his head back and forth, the barrel of the TAR 21 he held at his right side angled down. Without turning, he motioned with his left hand. A second soldier emerged from the vehicle, pulling a listless Aisha by one arm. A third soldier got out after her and took her other arm. Together they hurried with her toward the shelter where they dropped her down on the short bench. The soldiers then returned to the vehicle, which spun around, spitting gravel in its wake, and headed back the way it had come.

Aisha remained sitting, slumped over, barely taking in her surroundings. She wasn't sure where she was. The slight morning chill bit into her; she pulled the shawl tight. Her head began to sag with drowsiness. She shook her head back and forth to clear it and mustered the strength to stand up by supporting her weight against one of the advertising panels that formed the shelter's wall. She hadn't slept for she didn't know how long, and somewhere inside her she felt hungry, very hungry. The pain in her empty stomach was the only thing overcoming the urge to curl up and fall asleep on the concrete slab at her feet. She let the pain grow until the distraction was too much, and she pushed herself away from the ad and walked out of the shelter. She started to go left toward the checkpoint, but stopped, not wanting to see people, to hear voices, to have to speak, not wanting anything but home and her bed. She turned and took an uneven step, then regained her balance and began down the road in the direction home must be in, she was sure.

* * *

There was a new checkpoint on the old Nablus road north of Ramallah. That road was, like most, a narrow, gravel track, in poor condition, winding its way from village to village. It took hours to go ten kilometers on it. The checkpoint would just add to the delays. Idith had been assigned, along with two others, to monitor this checkpoint on a staggered schedule. She had started early and hoped to arrive on time.

Along the way, she had been thinking of America. Not America the superpower, the best ally of Israel, but the America where her daughter was, her daughter who had just emailed yesterday that she was going to have a third child. America, to Idith, was the land of her loss. But then, so was the land she was driving through now. Two faces of loss. Her children had left her here, forsaking their home. With regret, she knew. It hadn't been easy for them. But they had known that to put it off would make it worse. Idith had once worked in a nursery. Transplanting is easier on the young; older plants—and people—find it harder. She missed her daughter, and her daughter missed her, and both missed home, the home that had been. That was her loss, too. But her roots were too deep, she suspected, to take the risk of transplanting herself. Maybe later, if things got worse, the risk would be worth it, but not yet.

She had passed through the Qalandya checkpoint on the border with Israel and was heading north. But it was slow going. She poked along through village after village, passing slower vehicles when she could, but mostly stuck behind them. Her car was a dusty blue link in a creeping chain of cars, small trucks, and delivery vans, nearly touching each other at times, their pace picking up occasionally, only to slow to a near stop at each turn, each bump, each need for someone to put on his brakes, even for a second or two. Idith looked at her watch. She was going to be late, and there was nothing she could do about it. She started marking her progress against that of a woman wearing a shawl over her head who was walking on the side of the road, maybe fifty meters ahead. Idith would move closer, then as she was forced to slow or stop, the woman would open up a gap, which Idith would begin to close again as traffic began to move forward again. The figure would trip and stumble every now and again, limping for a few steps before regaining a regular if labored stride. A couple of times Idith saw the woman lose balance and only prevent herself from falling by slamming her hand down on whatever was nearest to support her: a building, a rock, a car. Even so, she fell once, lying motionless for two of Idith's heartbeats before pushing herself to her knees and then, with an effort, standing to her feet. Idith gradually drew even. The woman was younger than she had thought, and shifting her eyes to the sweat-streaked face, Idith recognized her. Idith leaned over the passenger seat and tried to get the woman's attention through the open passenger window.

"Get in."

The face did not look up.

"Please. Get in."

"No. Leave me alone."

"I know who you are. I'll take you home."

Aisha started to protest again, but closed her mouth before the words could come out. For a few moments she stared at Idith, her body rigid with stubbornness, but her whole frame soon bent over in resignation. She lowered her eyes, pulled open the door to Idith's car, and slumped down in the passenger seat.

"I live in Qalunya."

Aisha looked awful. She was filthy. Her hair hung in a stringy mass around her head, and there were deep grey smudges under her eyes. How long had it been since this girl had slept?

"Are you all right?"

Idith wanted to ask more, but Aisha's eyes, barely open, were staring down at nothing, and Idith understood that now was not the time for questions, or answers.

A few minutes later, Aisha said, in a tired, distant voice, "Thank you for taking me home." Idith moved the car forward as the line surged and stopped, surged and stopped. At the next fork, Idith made a quick decision and turned onto a less-traveled road that ran westward, toward Qalunya. After a few minutes she glanced over at Aisha. The girl was asleep.

Idith had heard that Aisha had been taken and was surprised she had been released so soon. But these things were often unpredictable, almost matters of caprice, like a sudden storm that pelted you for a few minutes and then was gone, leaving a dead space before life got back to normal. It was like this when people disappeared. They were there; they were gone; then after days or weeks or months, they were there again. It was all disorienting, for the victims, for

216

their families, and maybe that was the point. It was hard to think of another reason. The young men became resentful; she had seen it, heard it. But it also created in many of them a malaise, a sense of being out of place. They had been plucked out of their surroundings, held in limbo, and returned, but it was a transplanting of a kind. Their roots sometimes could not regain hold of the earth, and they withered. That's what it was, she thought. Inside, they just dried up. What they did to regain themselves varied. Some turned to protest, organized or not, and when it became violent, they were picked up again or went into hiding. Or they left. Some just left to begin with, or tried to.

Some filled their void with God. This she understood; religion in this part of the world had always been an identity, but seldom a choice. So God was a familiar place to sink your roots deeper. But you can't sink roots in the infinite, only in concrete parts of it. And which ones? She had seen it often enough on the other side of the wall, people rooted in a God she could not recognize. This was her despair, and, much to her husband's dismay, she seldom went to temple. And when she did, she never opened her mouth. Her voice never sounded, never resonated inside the walls any more. She had found she couldn't sing a note. Not in there, not in a viewless cage. It saddened her, but even parts of her own country gave her the same feeling, like she was in a darkened place where the only light was filtered through thick, colored, distorted glass, and she couldn't see out.

That light, the light of religion. She should have wanted it, she knew. She should have let it cover her, let it be what illuminated her life, her world. She just hadn't. She knew also that now it was too late. She knew the glass changed it, altered the outside light. So she had begun coming here to the West Bank, where there was no filter for the light, and where what she saw disturbed her more every day. If the light of religion dismayed her, the light of God tore her apart.

She shook off all this thinking. It was too much. She needed to focus on the road and getting Aisha back home.

* * *

"You released her? Why?"

The door had slammed against the wall and made a divot in the sheetrock. Andrei decided to let his junior officer vent.

"Orders."

Andrei looked up at Joshua.

"They were very clear: 'Let her go immediately. No arguments.'"

This wasn't true. Andrei had made the decision himself. But he didn't want any crap from Joshua. It was his call to make, and he had made it.

"But we were so close!"

"To what? Give me a break, Josh. You worked on that girl for three days and got nothing except circles under your eyes. She's clean and you know it."

"No Arab is clean. You know *that*," responded Joshua, still agitated. "They all have contacts with *someone*. They're all involved, in one way or another."

"Some are. Some aren't. We're looking for facts, not confirmation of our prejudices. Leave that to the politicians." He looked at the younger man. "My gut told me she was clean, and we weren't going to get much of anything out of her. I trust my gut."

"But she's the leader! Look at what she has done! People are throwing rocks at the wall in one place, shooting at it in another. It's out of hand, and it's embarrassing us. She should have been locked up and forgotten."

"No." Andrei shook his head, trying to be patient. "She's just nuts. Can't you see that? More of a symbol than a leader. Harmless for the time being, probably harmless period. We know who really calls the shots over there, and it's no girl schoolteacher. It's just a matter of time before we get signs of their pulling the strings. The girl's a distraction. I mean that. Anyway, keep up the good work and don't let minor shit interfere with the job."

He looked down and started flipping the sheets of a small pile of papers in front of him.

Dismissed, Joshua turned and left. He took care to close the door quietly behind him.

Andrei lifted his eyes just enough to see the door close, then sat back a second. Joshua was young, but his suspicions were based on a good deal of experience nonetheless. He headed a team of interrogators that had broken some very stubborn cases—hardened terrorists. He used the whole range of interrogation options, some less pleasant than others, but he got results, solid, reliable results. Trouble was, Joshua liked things to be clear and liked to make sure things stayed that way. Jew, Arab. Us, them. Good, bad. It was the easy simplicity of the young. Convinced of themselves, pushing ahead with not a second's hesitation. Andrei remembered being the same way. And then life tripped him up and kept tripping him. Oh, how he had loved breathing the fire of righteous conviction! So sure of everything. Not any more. For him it had been a burned-out house in Lebanon. He had no idea whose it was. Some Muslim, maybe a Druze. It didn't matter and you couldn't tell, anyway. A house was a house, anyone could live in it, just as long as you took care of it. He had been blooded—killed people, walked right by more corpses than he could remember. No problem there. A dead enemy is a good enemy. But that house had stayed with him. Perhaps because it had been such an old house. It had stood for a long time, settled in the land, comfortable with it, contributing to it. Nothing like sterile new construction. And one of our shells had blasted it to bits. A good house. A solid house. With land and a garden. Not any more.

To hell with it. He was getting maudlin. A sure sign of age. He was losing his edge, his clarity. His ruthlessness. He wondered if he was still doing his job.

This girl had been a strange case. Not all there. Just following some sort of weird compulsion. He'd sat through the interrogations. No red flags. No alarm bells. She was no threat. He felt sorry for her. He shouldn't feel sorry, not for any Arab. They were the enemy, all of them. Better they were dead or gone. He knew that. But occasionally, in his own house, with its own very tidy garden, he would think of that old house and feel its ghost around him. No, that wasn't right. He meant spirit. He didn't believe in ghosts; ghosts couldn't do anything to you. They were dead.

He wasn't supposed to have pity for the girl. It wasn't like him. And he didn't think he did. He just wanted her out of here. She interfered with his work. That was a more accurate assessment. She was a distraction for himself and his men. Better to get rid of her, get rid of the whole issue. Andrei realized he was taking a risk, but he saw little justification in keeping her locked up.

It was the correct move. This girl was just a little village figurehead—don't turn her into any sort of martyr. Let her fail publicly; the old men over there—the string pullers— they would see to that. Don't create a legend behind bars—a female Nelson Mandela in the West Bank, that they didn't need. These sorts of protests never lasted anyway. In the end, they produced mostly apathy, as they always turned out to be nothing but naïve, futile gestures. Soon, predictably enough, the pattern would revert to normal, as the Arabs went back to their typical mode of expression: acquiescence for most, violence for some. And that made things easier. That he and his men could deal with. Violence permitted control. Then things got simple for a while, just as Joshua saw them.

He sighed. It was all just a slog. He took both hands and tapped the edges of the stack of files in front of him to make a nice, neat pile, then took the top file and opened it.

Chapter 12

Idith knew Miryam was going to be annoyed at her for not showing up at their assigned checkpoint, but right now she had a different problem: how to get Aisha back home. It was going to take a long time; she knew that. The twenty kilometers or so would take hours, even by the most direct route. But she wasn't sure that was available. There were checkpoints everywhere. She had a list of them, though it was a week old. She pulled over to look at it. In a few minutes, after checking, she was reasonably sure there was a way to Qalunya that was clear, though it would be slow. It was possible to avoid checkpoints if you were willing to drive far out of your way. If there were any new flying checkpoints, she would just have to deal with them.

She pulled back onto the road. At al-Manshiyya, she would take a farmer's road to Summayl. After a little while on the Jamassin road, she would cross through a dilapidated vineyard that a young man was trying to rebuild. She had met him at a checkpoint. His truck had been turned away and she had bought a bottle of his wine out of sympathy. Since then she had passed by a few other times, eating dinner once with him and his family. He wouldn't mind the trespass.

She wondered if Aisha had her identity papers on her. Probably not. The authorities wouldn't have been that generous. Without those papers, Aisha wouldn't be able to get through one checkpoint, let alone two. She would wake her in a while to ask. In the meantime, Idith drove. For more than an hour her car crept along the road behind delivery trucks, going so slowly that Idith didn't bother to avoid the potholes. She just let the car sink into them and clamber out, up and down, over and over, as the dust of midday rose and made it even harder to breathe in the heat. A little relief came when she finally was able to leave the road for a pitted gravel path that led across an olive grove, behind old stone houses, passing by backyards, trash cans, tool sheds. The engine groaned in low gear, but soon they were on a better track, then another road. At the turnoff for the vineyard, Aisha began to move. Her eyes fluttered and a soft moan meant she had woken up.

Idith pulled over.

"How are you feeling?"

The eyes finally focused, as Aisha took in where she was.

"I'm all right."

Idith reached into the back seat and opened a small cooler.

"You hungry?"

"No." A breath taken. "Yes."

"Bread and cheese. Not much, but take all you want. There's water, too."

Aisha ate. Idith watched her. Aisha chewed slowly, though she had to be famished. She took a water bottle and drank half of it at once, looking embarrassed when she finished for the sounds she made.

"Sorry."

"Don't worry about it."

"Thanks."

Aisha looked at Idith now.

"You said you knew who I was."

"Yes. I have seen you throw the stones. Many times."

"You know what we are doing?"

"I was told about the missile attack, yes."

"You know who the people who throw the rocks are?"

"They live in your village."

"They are related to the children. Or knew them. There is a connection. We all share something."

Idith steered around a curve in the road.

"Lots of people watch you."

"Yes. Why do they?"

"You don't know?"

225

"Why do you watch?"

The car lurched as it hit a large rock, and Idith yanked the steering wheel hard left to stay on the road.

"I need to watch where I am going." Idith smiled, then turned thoughtful again. "I'll have to think about that. I just like it. It moves me, but I can't say why exactly. I'll have to think about it."

Their car was now stuck behind a truck ascending a small hill in low gear. They slowed to a walking pace.

"A lot of people come."

Aisha sat still for a few moments, not looking at Idith.

"Yes. I don't know why. They just come."

The truck pulled aside at the top of the hill to let them pass, and they picked up speed. They rode to the next village without saying anything.

The shadows of the buildings and trees were at their smallest; the heat of the day was peaking. As they passed through the village, the dust hung over the road and even with all the windows open, the car was stifling. A kilometer or so beyond the village, the traffic, which had been moving along steadily, stopped, and Idith, breaking the brief, warm lull that had descended over her, swore to herself. They were coming to a checkpoint. It would be difficult to turn around. The road was too narrow here, with banks rising sharply on both sides, and the traffic was bumper to bumper. Idith stuck her head out the window and looked ahead. The barrier was simple, just a wooden bar across the road. She could see three soldiers standing in front of it; there might be more. All looked young. Two of the soldiers were talking in louder and louder tones with a truck driver.

The truck would be forced to turn around. How, she couldn't imagine, but they would force him. This was how it went.

The argument was getting quite heated now. The driver had gotten out of his truck's cab and was clearly angry, gesturing wildly with his hands and arms. It looked like he was carrying food of some kind, vegetables maybe. Something that would rot if it wasn't sold. Maybe he would try a different route and try to get past the checkpoints there, or maybe he would try to sell it locally, instead of where he was going. The price would drop. He had no real choice. He may as well have been driving a donkey cart a thousand years ago, for this was the effect. He was being sent back—back on the road, back in time.

Idith turned around in her seat and found the old black sweater she usually left there. It was thick and long, for when she was out late and the temperature dropped, which it did at night in these hills.

"Aisha! Get down on the floor and cover yourself with this as well as you can."

Not waiting for a response, Idith got out of the car and fished her Machsom Watch ID out of her pocket. Holding it in front of her, she walked toward the nearest soldier. He was very young; he couldn't have been in the army all that long.

She hoped she looked like his grandmother.

"Stop!"

She did as he ordered. His rifle remained pointed at her, but its barrel dropped slightly as he approached.

"What do you want?"

"I'm Israeli, with the Watch. I'm assigned to the checkpoint about five kilometers farther on, and I'm late. Is there any way you can move this along?"

His cheeks tightened; his mouth became a thin line. It was doubtful he was a friend of the Watch.

"Why don't you go back to your car and wait? Shouldn't be too long."

She knew what that meant.

"Or I can station myself here for the day. Your choice."

The soldier took her ID and examined it, taking far longer than was necessary. But they always did. Standard procedure. She was not welcome. Also normal.

He looked up, returned her ID and then looked down the road, past the checkpoint.

"Go ahead." He turned his head toward the other soldiers. "Moishe! Let this woman pass. She's with the Watch. Wants to be on her way."

The soldier he was yelling to waved back and moved to raise the barrier.

"Thank you."

As she sprinted back to her car, Idith knew that everyone in the line would hate her in about ten seconds. She got in.

Aisha was huddled as far down as she could. Idith straightened the sweater and pulled out, scraping the car ahead of her.

"Israeli bitch!" spat a voice in Arabic from its front seat.

"Let's hope this works."

Moishe had raised the barrier. Idith started driving slowly, then picked up enough speed to make looking into her car a little more difficult and passed by the barrier. Once past, she kept her speed, raising a healthy cloud of dust. She only slowed down as she approached the next village a few kilometers later.

"You can get up now. We're through."

"Thanks."

"Don't thank me just yet."

An hour later, though, Idith was breathing more calmly. She was fairly sure now there would be no more checkpoints.

Aisha stiffened abruptly in her seat.

"What time is it?"

Idith glanced at the clock readout below the tachometer.

"A little after three."

"Take me to the wall."

"Don't you want to go home first?"

A smile appeared. The first.

"If I do that my mother won't let me leave."

"She's right."

"Can I borrow your cell phone? I need to call her."

Idith fished the phone out of her inner pocket and handed it to Aisha, who then dialed a number slowly.

"Mom? It's me."

Idith could hear shrieks and a string of babbled syllables come through the earpiece. Aisha held the phone at almost arm's length until the sounds stopped.

"No, I'm fine. I'll be home in an hour or so."

Another string of syllables, high pitched, rising.

"Someone's driving me. An Israeli woman."

Aisha's head moved up and down to the next burst from the phone.

"I'll tell you about it later."

Aisha had the phone to her ear now.

"No, really. I'm fine. I'm not hurt. I'll see you in an hour. Please tell Father. Bye."

She handed the phone back to Idith.

"Thank you."

Ten minutes later, Idith pulled the car off the road at the foot of the olive grove.

She had never really looked closely at the wall. From here, what was it? Ugly. It was ugly. The word jumped into Idith's mind and stuck there. Here, standing in the shadow it cast, she could see the wall's surface pockmarked with thousands of little scars. Pustules revealing its affliction. The disease that had been festering within it for so long had finally broken into the open, and, now, despite its mass, the wall was diminished.

Aisha was still in the passenger seat. The window was down, there was air now, a little breeze, but Aisha hadn't opened the door. Idith looked at her.

"Why do you do it?"

"Huh?"

"Why do you do it?"

"I have to."

"What will you accomplish?"

"Nothing."

"Nothing?"

"That's right. Nothing. I will accomplish nothing. Nothing is my accomplishment."

"I don't understand."

"I mean I'm not trying to accomplish anything. I have no expectation, no hopes, no dreams. I just have to do it. "

"Well, the wall is different. You have done that."

"It's just more obvious now."

"That's something."

"Not much. Not enough."

"Enough for what?"

"Maybe if I knew I could tell you. But I don't, so I can't."

"How long will you continue?"

"Until I know I don't have to do it anymore."

"Do you have any idea when that will be?"

"No. Not soon. I am sure of that. Not soon."

"I'm surprised you can still keep doing it."

"I would be surprised if I could stop."

Aisha had been spotted and now people surrounded the car, shouting, crying out. Aisha sighed and opened the door, at once bombarded with questions, hands reaching to touch her, arms trying to embrace her, faces wanting to kiss her. Aisha submitted to it, speaking little but assuring people she was all right. She said nothing about what had happened, just that she was fine.

Gradually she made her way to the wall. The throwers lined up and the ritual began. Twelve stones were thrown, twelve names were called. As she eased back her arm to make the last, silent throw, Aisha stopped and turned around. She stretched out her arm and pointed straight at Idith. Idith shivered. She felt exposed. People turned to look where Aisha was pointing. Idith saw the expressions, some confused, others severe. Clearly a Jew. Was Aisha accusing her of something? Then the hand turned over and beckoned her.

She heard a man's voice from close by.

"She wants you."

Idith got out of the car and walked toward where Aisha was standing, toward the wall. She felt the wall rise above her, and she felt cold in the heat. She reached Aisha, and Aisha held out her hand. There was a stone in it.

"Take this."

"I can't."

"Take it and throw it with the rest"—Aisha stepped

closer and each word she spoke was unhurried—"You need to. I know you need to."

Aisha turned to face the wall, stared at its ugliness for several long moments, then, with a sudden, swift movement, cast her stone at the ravaged gray surface. The others in the line hurried to follow. Aisha looked at Idith.

"Throw it."

As stones clattered against the face of the wall, Idith felt her mind go blank, and the motion of her arm filled her body as she sent the stone in her hand arcing away from her. It hit with a little crack; its echo lingered in the air longer than Idith thought it could.

"Walk with me."

Aisha accompanied Idith to her car.

"I'll walk from here."

"Are you sure?"

"I have to."

* * *

Waking a few hours later, Aisha was disoriented for a moment by her surroundings, but glad, after a disconcerting but short pause, to recognize the disheveled figures next to her as her parents, who themselves had slept little and looked it. A doctor later came by and was able to reassure them all that Aisha was suffering from a little dehydration and exhaustion from her ordeal, but that was it. A few days of rest and sleep and she would be back to normal.

Shortly after midday the next day, a small convoy of official-looking cars pulled up outside, and a fastidiously dressed man was escorted by several armed men into the house. He shook the hands of Hana and Khalid.

Aisha appeared at the door to her bedroom. The man motioned them all to sit on the couch, then took a chair and positioned himself directly in front of Aisha.

"Teacher," he said, addressing her with formal deference, "my name is Fayez Sayigh." He took for granted she knew who that was. Often known by his nom de guerre, Abu Nadir, Sayigh was a member of the central committee of Fatah. "How are you feeling?"

"I'm well enough."

Aisha's words were slow, without inflection. Abu Nadir looked at her with an eye practiced in political calculation.

"Teacher," he said again, "let me first say how much I respect you for what you have been doing." His voice was measured, and he paused again, looking her in the eyes. She turned away and fixed her eyes on the bedclothes. "We have, of course, sent an official protest to the Israeli prime minister about your abduction. But, as you probably can imagine, I doubt there will even be a response, much less an apology."

Aisha adjusted herself on the couch and focused on scratching a bit of dirt from her palm.

"It has been quite interesting to watch you." Now her eyes darted back to him. He smiled at her. "Oh yes, we have

234

been watching your little, well, what is it now exactly?" A brief flicker of perhaps genuine concentration crossed his face, then he waved his hand as if batting the thought away. "In any case, your activities have gotten quite a response. More and more people come each day, I am told."

Her face said nothing to him. He tried to look closer at her, but she turned away again.

"And the Israelis have noticed too. But I guess you know that. Can you tell me what they wanted?"

"The same thing you do." She looked away again and the listlessness returned to her voice.

"Oh? And what would that be?"

She took a long breath.

"You all want to know why."

He gave a nod, and when he spoke he tried to make sure he sounded concerned for her above all else.

"So let me ask, why are you doing this? What are you trying to prove?"

"Nothing."

"Is that what you told the Israelis?"

"They didn't believe me either."

"I would like you to speak with our people about your interrogation with the Israelis. Perhaps we can learn something."

"No. I just want to rest."

Abu Nadir nodded as if the question had been unimportant to begin with.

"Very well. I understand totally. But you realize, this sort of thing will continue."

Aisha's mother stifled a sharp "No!" Abu Nadir turned to her and smiled, as if to reassure her.

"No, Umm Abdul, I don't mean being kidnapped in the middle of the night again, not necessarily anyway."

He looked back at Aisha, who met his eyes again with an expressionless stare. "I think the Israelis must think that was a mistake. Otherwise, my child,"—his voice took on a paternalistic air, the official gravitas he liked to affect when speaking to the public—"you would probably still be in custody. No, I mean people will watch you, as they have been, but it will get more—what? Obvious? You are attracting attention, and I think people are wondering just what you might be up to and where it will lead."

"I'm not doing anything. I don't want anything. I want to be left alone. Everyone should go away and leave me alone."

"Oh, I think it is too late for that. And really, what do you expect? You lead maybe hundreds of people in some sort of protest and you don't want anything? I myself find that hard to believe."

"I don't care! You're all the same. Leave me alone!"

She had been sitting up straight, leaning toward him, and now fell back on the couch, drained by her outburst.

"Aisha!"

Abu Nadir held up his hand to calm Hana.

"She is upset. No matter. It is understandable. What we have, however, is a situation, a situation that must not be allowed to get out of control. You have created this for whatever reason, and there is no doubt people look to you as a leader. Because of that, both I and the prime minister are concerned about your security. Things will only get worse. Obviously, you will continue what you are doing, I don't expect you to do otherwise, but I would like to suggest that we provide you with a detachment from our National Security Force for your protection, around the clock, of course."

"No."

Aisha's voice was firm. Abu Nadir chose not to argue.

"Very well, perhaps your parents can speak to you later." He reached into his pocket. "Here is my card. If I can be of service, please call me." He stood. "I strongly urge you to accept my offer. Whether you like it or not, you have become a leader, and being a leader isn't always easy"—he paused for effect—"or safe."

A small crowd had gathered in front of the house, attracted by the arrival of the convoy. As Abu Nadir left the house, he waved as he walked to the lead SUV, which had already started its engine. As the convoy pulled away, several in the crowd glared at the vehicles as if to blame them for everything.

Chapter 13

Idith spent the next few days at the checkpoint on the Nablus road. Slow and deliberate, hurrying for no one, the soldiers methodically checked identification papers and permits. The line of people and vehicles stretched out and time slowed, as if the present were being pulled out of reach, back into the past. One man being turned away started arguing loudly with a soldier. He was immediately handcuffed and made to sit on the ground by the side of the road. Later, after he had cooled down, he was released. From what Idith could gather, he was a baker and starting a new job, but his documents had not been updated. She did not see him again. Perhaps he had been able to get through elsewhere; perhaps he had lost the job and there was no point in coming this way any more.

Life descended into the vulnerabilities of the past: a woman gave birth in a car after hours of waiting; an old man had a heart attack in front of Idith. He survived, but only just. This checkpoint can't halt life any more than the others do, she thought.

What was it that pulsed in these hills? She could look around and see land that had not changed in many, many centuries. What ancient gods were still lurking there? The soldiers at the checkpoint moved in a manner as set and formal as priests. The barrier was their altar and the long lines of waiting people, supplicants. The checkpoint was a temple to something. She wondered what.

At the end of the week, Idith was able to come to the ritual again. She was tired and might have gone straight home to do some cleaning and straightening, domestic tasks that had been neglected since she had joined the Watch, but she found herself, without fully deciding to, on the roads, making the turns to get to the ritual. Because the crowds had gotten so much larger, she had to park farther away, on a side street in the village down the road, and it now took several minutes of walking before she could begin to climb up to her usual viewing spot. Letting the heat of the afternoon and rhythm of her steps muffle everything but the feel of the ruts in the path, she was startled when a hand touched her shoulder. A man stood behind her and gestured down the hill to where Aisha was standing, looking up at her. The man gestured again, and Idith nodded. When she had descended to level ground, Aisha took her by the hand and walked her to a space in the throwing line. From a pocket in her skirt, Aisha took out a little bag and held it out to her. Idith knew the bag contained thirteen stones.

Idith wanted to refuse; she was out of place here, a spectator only. It was she who was being watched now, she could feel it. An intruder. But as she raised her eyes to the wall, that self-consciousness evaporated. She took the bag. She felt her active mind empty itself, as if it had to let something else in. She felt in the bag and withdrew a stone. She ran her fingers over it, felt its texture, its weight. It was heavy in her hand, heavier than she thought it could be.

Then came the cry from Aisha, "Ahmad!" Idith waited, then shouted with the rest. Her body flowing with the rest, she launched her stone. The wind, which had risen, kicking up spirals of dust, carried the name upward to the watchers on the hill. Its breeze swathed her as she took the second stone. "Nassim!" Each echo faded into the next throw, binding them. And after the twelfth stone had been thrown, she held the thirteenth in her hand and waited to call another name, silently. And with one motion, they all launched their last stone, only this time the names were silent, and all different. Idith had screamed a name to herself and now had tears streaking her face. The name had been her own.

* * *

Idith moved slowly away with the crowd, stumbling just a bit as she tried to wipe dirt from her eyes. What had that been?

She choked on some dust in her throat and stopped to bend over and cough it loose. The wind—what was the wind doing? Why did it behave that way? Wind. The word was *ruach* in Hebrew, a language she had learned along with the rest of her generation when they and their country were young. She stopped and whirled around, knocking into a tall man. She didn't look at him, but walked fast, back to the spot from which she had thrown the stones. Gasping, sweating by the time she got there, she turned and surveyed the scene. The space around her in front of the wall was empty now, and she could only see what had happened in her mind's eye. But she could feel the wind on her face. "*Ruach,*" she said aloud. "*Ruach Elohim.*" She said it softly several times. And shook her head, as if not believing what she was saying. The wall stretched out before her in both directions. Imposing. Immutable. No, that wasn't right, for its face was altered here. The pocks and gouges were deeper here, a malignant rash spreading out in each direction. The wall had indeed changed. A little. To her. Shaking her head once more, she headed back in the direction where her car was parked. As she entered the tangle of streets and houses in the village that lay beyond the hill with the olive grove, she noticed a tall man standing in the shadow of a building. She was still muttering to herself. She realized that it was the man she had bumped into, and she quickened her pace to get by.

Hussein did not move, but watched the woman as she passed and listened to what she was repeating to herself. She looked distraught and confused. A small Jewish woman, what was she doing here? And what was she saying, over and over again? The phrase puzzled him. He understood it perfectly well; he had learned Hebrew while in an Israeli prison years ago. "*Ruach Elohim,*" he repeated. *Ruach* meant wind, he knew, but it also meant spirit. *Ruach Elohim. Ruhullah* in Arabic. Spirit of God. It was a powerful, sacred phrase in both languages. She was blaspheming, certainly. But this thought did not convince him.

* * *

Hussein was walking back to the safe house again, following the same route, which he knew was doubly unwise. But he had to think and walking alone was the best way to do that. The girl Aisha had surprised him by proving him wrong. She was stubborn, and perhaps he should have seen that in her. He had seen men broken by interrogation, diminished, shamed. Surely a few nights in a cell would have taught her the hopelessness of what she was doing. But a bigger surprise was that he realized it pleased him that he had been wrong. And this was unsettling. He was not often wrong. This was simply because now, at this stage of life, he reserved judgment on many things, maybe most things. And those times when he was wrong, he accepted the fact without emotion, keeping his distance. He had learned not to invest himself in right or wrong too much. Not as he had once

242

done. And being right was merely a fact as well, not an occasion for anything else, other than moving on to the next problem. But now, he felt glad he had been wrong, glad that the little teacher was still at it, doing her futile little dance. But now he saw something more to it. A relentlessness. He had to think about that.

But on this unwise walk back to the safe house, he found he was thinking not of her, but of himself. What was he? What had he become? The struggle, for him, was a bridge he was crossing. Or maybe he had already crossed it. Over to what? Resistance. It was all he had ever known or desired. It was his purpose. It was necessary. If you did not resist, you acquiesced, you surrendered. You failed. Failure was not death, it was annihilation, erasure. He could not allow that to happen; he owed his family, his people. But what was resistance? He was no longer sure. Was it metal and blood, machine and flesh, both spent, both wasted? He needed to take a sudden deep breath. And another.

Perhaps he was old. Old and soft. His passions were ebbing, and along with that, his discipline. Perhaps. He had no daughters, no children at all. Had that made him more rigid? Was that what age had done to him? Made him a parent, finally? And of whom? He regretted his choices. Often. He had not remarried. His loss at his wife's death had been too great. Or at least he had thought so at the time. He wasn't so sure now. What had he left for himself? He could marry. No doubt an arrangement could be made. But what would it mean to him? Not what it should have. Best to leave such things behind and concentrate on the future.

He envied this teacher in a way. She was inspiring people—clearly. Not just in her class. That had been shattered. But look at them. Every day. Every day they came, and watched her. Every day. What was it? What was this little teacher doing for these people?

He was himself a teacher in a way. Like her. Perhaps that was it. That's what he was seeing. He had schooled many recruits in his time, though the job now went to others. There was joy in teaching, getting someone to cross a threshold of knowledge. He had felt it. No doubt so had she. But perhaps her youth stoked more passion in her than his age could in him. And so she could continue, fresh for her daily exercise in futility, where he would have given up and turned to something that could show progress, tangible results. Tangible, yes. A word for accountants, not philosophers, to be sure. He smiled at his own hypocrisy. He knew the value of accountants, but their vision was limited to what could be put in a ledger. He had had to measure other things. Commitment, faith, dedication, piety, discipline. These things counted. They added up. To what? He was no longer sure. He had added up the intangibilities in men. Could he really claim to have accumulated anything?

He had come to count on things. Again the accountant's language. Counting on things. Like discipline. Propriety. Truth. God's truth. Certainty. He had to admit he needed that. But what had happened to his submission to the intangible? God was both, he thought. To accept God, he had to accept intangibility, too. Why couldn't he anymore? He had come to need certainty, and he had taught others to do so. But this was wrong. Life is not certain. Only God is certain, but God is intangible.

He smiled to himself, which was rare enough. The imams would smile with the aloof indulgence of the learned at his attempts to characterize God, and his "colleagues" in the movement (they narrowed their eyes at him when he called them that) would accuse him of blasphemy. God, they would say, is certainly tangible. They wouldn't mean it the same way, he didn't think, but they would agree on that. And maybe God is tangible. God is everywhere, in everything, so God was certainly in things we can see and touch. So God is tangible and intangible at the same time. A contradiction in terms. A logical fallacy, as one of his old teachers often liked to say about his students' efforts to explain the world. His moment of humiliation had come with regard to a paper he had written once for history class. No, not humiliation, humility. Humiliation is disgrace, humility is a gift, a rare gift. The topic had been something to do with colonialism, an easy target for a committed mind. He had given a long rant on the depredations of the British, with their white suits, haughty language, and ridiculous afternoon tea. But he had not finished when his professor stopped him. "Now argue the other side," he had told him. After trying with all the indignation he could muster to protest that there was no legitimacy to the other side's case, Hussein came up with an argument. It was weak, but he had to admit to himself, not completely untruthful. "Open both eyes to the world, not just one," was all the professor had said.

A contradiction in terms. That made sense enough to him, actually. Life was a contradiction in terms so why wouldn't God be? He supposed that the only thing he could confidently say about God was that God was infinite, like the universe, and therefore contained infinite aspects, infinite possibilities, infinite quandaries for the human mind. His colleagues wouldn't like that much, either. They liked their God tangible, concrete. Tangible—there was that word again —enough so they could be sure of absolute confidence in their understanding.

He wondered if all this thinking about God was a sign of age, at least the way he was thinking of God. When he was younger, God was much sharper, clearer in his mind. These days all he could do was wonder, which was what he was doing now. When did all this wondering begin? He wasn't sure. He had always been curious about things at school, annoying the teachers with his peppered questions. All his life he had sought answers. And he had usually found them. At least in school. He had graduated from university feeling wonderfully full of the confidence of knowledge. But he hadn't found an interesting answer in a long time. He solved little problems, sure, but not big ones. Maybe because, like

God, the biggest problems were infinite, or close enough to it.

He wasn't sure he had the energy to take them on any more. At least not with confidence. You lose confidence with age, if you have any humility. Life makes you humble. It had made him humble. And this was what God wanted. Humility. It was in the Book. He thought it might be in all the books. But if humility meant loss of confidence, loss of the conviction, the assuredness that confidence gave you . . . well, another bit of failed logic.

He was getting lost in words. What he meant, he realized, was that confident knowledge told you what the truth was, and as he had aged, this had slipped away. Humility had been forced upon him, and he no longer knew any truth. He couldn't find it; he couldn't recognize it, he was sure. Almost sure. He smiled at himself again. This was a strange day.

Chapter 14

Karim Shaath held the stone and closed his eyes. He thought of Jamal, the name he was about to speak. A child he never knew. He thought of other Jamals: one who worked in a garage owned by his father, his hands stained with grease and oil, permanently it seemed, already at the age of nineteen; one who was at university studying Arabic poetry, a subject his father, dead last year of a heart attack at age forty-six, had thought useless; one who had blown himself up in Tel Aviv four years ago, killing five women, three children, and an old man; and one who was now five years old and the apple of his grandfather's eye. That Jamal's grandfather now opened his eyes and threw the stone hard with everyone else, and yelled with everyone else, "Jamal," except that his voice seemed to scream rather than yell, and his elbow snapped with pain when he let the stone loose.

The stone hit the wall with hundreds of others. In the few days since Aisha's return, the line had grown much longer. It stretched so far in both directions that Karim had no idea how many voices, how many hands, had just spat their frustration at the faceless mass that loomed over them. His place was maybe four hundred meters down the line, near where the olive grove ended and the wall approached a few low apartment buildings. The rocks pelted the barrier, the heavy clatter rolling into the distance, growing fainter until silence filled the void again. The bits of concrete chipped away by the impacts dropped, spent, onto a growing heap at the barrier's foot. After weeks of their coming here every day, the wall was now chipped and scarred up its entire height. He remembered when it was smooth and new, when his memories of what was behind it were sharp. So long ago. The wall had cut a jagged swathe through his ancient village, an unnatural, inorganic growth among the small houses, yards, and gardens that hadn't changed since Karim was young, and long before that. It had stood there, a high, forbidding blankness where a landscape had been. The wall was over four times as tall as the tallest man. One could not hope to see over it without backing up and climbing to the roof of a building, and that was unwise, as Israeli snipers were ever watchful for any movement that could be taken for potential rocket launching. No, rooftops were not safe anywhere near the wall. So in the years since the wall was erected, what was behind it had become the stuff of nostalgia and legend—and regret. Karim could remember the old olive trees, so many, covering several hillsides, unavoidable when you raised your eyes from your work. They had filled your view. And like in so many villages, they had always been there, or so he had thought, so he continued to think in his memory. But he also remembered the settlement that had appeared one day on the hill a few months before the wall. It had been a couple of buses, some trailers, and a hastily erected barbed-wire fence, right on top of the hill, amid the trees, almost hidden by them at first, and he wondered if the trees had survived it, or if the settlement had grown to swallow them. He wondered what would greet his eyes now if he raised them. He was not sure he wanted to imagine.

The last stone, the silent stone, was always heaviest in his hand. He wasn't sure why. Perhaps because there were so many more unspoken names it bore. Perhaps because the other names had tired him so. Sometimes he had a thought in his mind, a memory, and gave it to this stone to carry with it. As brief as it was, the stone's journey seemed long, a cycle of effort and exhaustion without end or significance. Today he had no thought. He rubbed the stone with his thumb, feeling its grit, its weight. Then he threw, and as the stone flew toward the wall, his fingers curled around the empty space in his palm, as if the stone were still there, loosening only at the crack of the stone against the wall.

Karim let his arm drop to his side with all the others. The light slap of skin against cloth, repeated down the line, echoing for a moment, then . . . stillness. The hundreds of human forms remained motionless. Karim's arm hurt, and he felt tired. It was the last stone; they were done for today. Tomorrow they would return. He had been doing this for weeks. It had grown mechanical, certainly, but somehow it was vital to him. Many of those he knew encouraged him to stop. He was too old. They felt it was pointless, yet he felt in the rhythm of what they were doing the pulse of something alive. He didn't know what, really, but something he knew he couldn't let go of, because to stop now would be to let it die, and with it, his memories, his ghosts. And then what would he be?

Feet scuffed in the dirt, each person's form turning around at its own speed, in its own manner, disbanding from the others now that they had finished. There was still a silence heavy on them, the space taken by the shouting of the names filling only slowly again with the little noises of what was left of the day. People walked away from the wall, groups formed and the sound of voices began to rise. Karim stayed where he was, taking in the vast pitted surface before him. He did this often. He felt the pressure of its mass, its malignancy, as it stood there, dormant for now, but still self-satisfied in its achievement. He did not want to turn his back on it too soon. He stared up at it and hated it.

Finally, he lowered his eyes and began to move toward home. He was tired, but the walk back would rejuvenate him as he took in the children playing in the streets and petted the dogs that dutifully challenged him with their barks, doing their job but looking for an affectionate friend and maybe a handout, always.

He had gone a few meters and his feet were about to touch the elongated shadow of the nearest building when he turned He didn't know why. The section of the wall just opposite him was moving. Impossibly, it was falling toward him. He backed up, though he was in no danger. The giant slab slapped the earth with a force that sent a shockwave rippling through the air and the earth. He could feel the impact on his face, in his feet. But the sound was muffled, soft even, as if the slab had simply given in to exhaustion from the effort of standing. Now it lay before him, prostrate. Karim wanted to run to it, to touch it. But there was a sharp, grating sound. The slabs on either side lurched and groaned and began to fall, pulled off balance by the first, and the two on the outside began to move as well. Then they collapsed, one on top of another, pieces breaking off and sliding to the ground, where they sank deep into the earth, unable to move. Dust rose and enveloped him, then blew away. Karim wiped the grit from his face. There was nothing in front of him now but a dead pile of concrete waste, crushed and defeated by its own weight.

Karim walked down to where he had been. Others who, like him, had also witnessed this, walked down to the wall as well. Some knelt, others prostrated themselves and began to pray. Karim just stood, taking in what lay beyond.

Through the gap in the wall, he could see the hillside. On the crest of the hill, where the ramshackle buses and trailers had been, there were now the utilitarian block-like buildings of a permanent settlement. But it was still small and clung, rather than sat, where it was, as if the buildings had not yet been able to set firm foundations, owing to resistance from the hill itself. A razor-wire fence was still twisted around the site, and as the low sun caught it, its angry light tried to fend off his view, but the fence only managed to reflect a yellow glare, the growling of an aging watchdog, fearful at any exposure of its encroaching weakness. Then it registered: the olive grove was still there, damaged perhaps, but alive. And as Karim took in the scene, the settlement seemed to recede beside the grove. The trees looked strong and green, almost youthful, and maybe even a bit taller. Maybe they had grown. And the settlement looked dirty and had a worn air, as if something had begun to eat at it from within, a growth sapping its strength, making it age before its time.

Now the leaves of the olive trees caught the light and began to outshine the wire. They moved in the breeze, sending beams of color at those staring across the broken concrete, as if to say yes, I am still here, I am alive.

Karim's memory embraced the panorama of the hillside. The faces of the men and women around him radiated, and they all stood still for a long time, drinking in the sustenance of the moment.

Karim became aware that others were arriving, drawn by the relayed shouts everywhere around him that the wall had fallen. As the rumor shattered into fact, into truth, Karim heard the cries—joyful cries of disbelief and exhilaration—and he felt the wind of shaking bodies with upraised arms racing past him toward the gap in the wall.

People were clambering over the fallen slabs of concrete, pointing and laughing, shouting defiantly. Some went so far as to cross over the pile and go to the other side, where they danced wildly, ecstatically, shrieking to empty their lungs. More people came down from the village and stopped, staring at the space in the wall through which the late afternoon light poured.

He heard the word *ayah*—a sign from God—uttered behind him; others said *mu'jiza*—miracle. He repeated *ayah* under his breath. But maybe the others were right. People had started dancing everywhere. Hundreds of men and women, many of whom had been throwing stones just a short while ago, returned and massed around the gap, dancing, singing. Some younger men arrived with their AK-47s and began shooting joyously in the air. Karim was grabbed by the hand and pulled into a circle of turning people, singing nonsensically, celebrating they knew not what, but something wonderful, miraculous, in a land where miracles had so long been absent.

The tear gas grenades came without warning. No one had heard the gunships approach until they were overhead.

The gas streamed through the crowd, which disbursed, coughing and gagging. Short bursts of gunfire sounded through the smoke, but these were scattered at best and remained unanswered as the gunships circled, their prop wash fanning the gas and driving the revelers back into the village, away from the opening in the wall.

Karim fled with the rest, coughing violently, stumbling down the narrow streets until the air lost the taste of the gas and he was free of its reach. He leaned against a wall and retched. His lungs burned, and he felt faint. For a long time he stayed there, breathing deeply, recovering. Finally, after the pain had ebbed, he stood up and started walking slowly back toward the olive grove. He would go to the top of the hill, away from the gas, and look through the gap until night obscured it. And he would come back tomorrow and watch it again, keep it in front of him so he didn't have to rely on memory again. He had done that for too long. As he made his way, unsteady and tentative with his steps, the olive grove on the hill filled his mind, and the certainty came to him that it was the grove itself—not just a symbol of life, but a force of life—that had broken the strength of the wall. And he knew then that the grove would outlast them all, and this salved both the ache of remembering and the sting in his eyes, and his steps became quicker and firmer.

* * *

As the last of the tear gas floated away, Dani and Zev pulled up at the gap in the wall in their jeep. The gunships would circle until a squad could arrive to erect a temporary barrier of razor wire. An engineering detachment would come tomorrow to assess the scene. Meanwhile, Dani and Zev grabbed their weapons and took a look for themselves. It was a mess. The concrete slabs had broken on top of one another, their huge fragments now littering a space about fifty meters wide.

They walked to the center of the gap, where the first slab had fallen.

"What the fuck?"

The earth was all churned up. It reminded Zev of the sea during a storm, peaks and valleys in the water, whitecaps flinging their froth into the wind. But here the sea was frozen into earth. The slabs weren't all broken. Some were intact, he thought. They had been spat out. Or great teeth had taken their foreign splinter and yanked them out. And they lay discarded now. Sweat dripped down his face, but Zev shivered.

"Someone really fucked up."

Zev turned to Dani.

"Why do you say that?"

"Well, these things didn't just fall over by themselves. Some damn engineer screwed up. Built them on unstable sand or something."

"I don't know."

"Can't be anything else, can it? All I know is, I don't want to be in the room when the fingers start pointing. What a mess!"

Zev shrugged and turned back to look through the gap in the wall. It was odd, standing on the ground, looking at all this from below instead of from above. He looked over at the slabs that were still standing. He and Dani were supposed to fill the gap in their ranks left by the fallen slabs? He found himself squaring his shoulders reflexively for a moment before shaking the thought loose. Here they were, he and Dani, with their gas masks and rifles, standing on slab corpses trying to look imposing for the crowd on the other side. He felt ridiculous. Tear gas still lingered in the air, but he could see the olive trees on the other side emerging from the haze. People had gathered where the air was clear, and some had moved back down toward the gap. They were looking straight at him. Well, no. They weren't. He could see their eyes; they were raised far past him. He turned around. There was the settlement the wall was supposed to protect, built on the hilltop next to another old olive grove. Zev saw a few armed settlers walking out in front of the wall meant to shield the collection of buildings behind it. He stepped toward them.

"You! You there! Get the hell out of here!"

The gas mask muffled his voice too much; it wouldn't carry. He took another few steps toward the men and flung his arm in an arc to make it clear that they should go back inside the settlement. The soldiers didn't need unreliable trigger fingers right now. He gestured again, and the settlers moved away, not completely out of sight, but far enough, he supposed.

Dani hadn't moved, but had kept facing the crowd. Zev turned back. They both held their weapons in front of them, the barrels pointed down. The crowd wasn't moving forward but was spreading out again.

"What do you think, Zev. We need to spray 'em again? Chopper's on standby."

"I'd wait, but it's your call."

"No sense having the brass think we haven't got any balls. We two can hold off a bunch of lousy Arabs. Like the Spartans at Thermopylae."

"Let's hope not."

Dani shaded his eyes with his hand.

"Nah. Not that bunch of faggots. Look at them. Scared stiff of us."

Zev squinted at the crowd. Their faces didn't look scared. They were just staring at the hill behind him. Instead of turning around, he looked at the hill of olive trees in front of him. The last trace of tear gas was gone, and the sun was just beginning to put the uppermost branches of the olive trees into silhouette. He watched; his mind emptied and let nothing in for a while. He felt safe. It was a strange feeling, and it made no sense to him at all.

Half an hour later, three trucks loaded with soldiers and razor wire pulled up behind them. An officer strode up and said he was relieving them.

* * *

Just as she had reached the schoolyard, Aisha felt something at her feet, a shudder, as the impact of the slabs hitting the earth reached her. The air became muffled, thick, and she had run back through it to the wall, across the olive grove, just as she had done the very first time. There were no thoughts within her, only the urgency of the moment, and when she reached the crest of the grove where she could finally see the wall, she stopped.

From the crown of the hill, Aisha could see the gap in the wall ringed in sunlight. The landscape beyond shone through. The shadows of the trees in the olive grove on the other side stretched out as if they were open arms of welcome, and she noticed that the shadows of the trees she stood among seemed to stretch out, too—impossibly— toward the trees out of view for so long. She couldn't move.

As people came and stared, she stayed where she was. Men and women, old and young streamed down the hillside and started to dance and sing—any song, nonsense songs, la la la, anything to make music. The tear gas had come quickly, suddenly; people had choked, and fled up to where she was, and they all could look back to see the olive grove on the other side, the settlement sitting uncomfortably next to it with little bunches of black-clothed figures staring back at them. A few people tried to approach the wire, only to turn away as more tear-gas grenades were lofted at them.

Now, the tear gas had dispersed and the soldiers had begun stringing razor wire across the gap. But the wire closed the gap to people, not to sight, and people were returning to the hill to look down from a safe distance. In a few minutes, a line of people formed along the crest of the hill among the olive trees, some standing, some sitting. All silent, their faces watching the gap below.

Karim came around the side of the hill and stopped to the left of Aisha. He was a little in front of her, and she could see his profile clearly against the sky. She tried to read his gaze as he surveyed the gap and the scene beyond, where an unfelt breeze was moving the branches of the olive trees on the hill ever so slightly. The noise and dust of the soldiers disappeared for the briefest of moments.

Without turning his head, he spoke.

"I grew up with those trees. Our house was just beyond the hill. I took my son there when he was little and showed him the best ones for climbing. When I have grandsons, I would like to take them there, too."

He turned to look at her.

"Tell me, which do they think is crueler, the barbed wire, which makes us bleed, or this view, which breaks our hearts?"

His voice had no emotion in it. Maybe his eyes did, she couldn't tell, for he turned his head toward the opening in the wall again, toward his olive grove.

They watched together until dusk, until the soldiers had finished stringing razor wire across the fallen concrete. A couple of television news crews pulled up on the road below. A reporter with a cameraman walked through the olive grove trying to find someone to interview, but no one would speak to him. The razor-wire barrier in place, the soldiers dug themselves in behind tiny sandbag fortresses for the night. As the sun set, all was still, and when the gap had turned dull and dark, Aisha turned and started her walk home. A crowd marched with her, singing, chanting, yelling, "Celebrate with us. Dance until the sun comes up!" But she declined. She wanted to walk alone tonight, in the hills, and smile up into the stars for a while.

Chapter 15

The crowds had been growing all day. IDF Command ordered several new checkpoints set up on the roads leading to Qalunya and its neighboring villages, but to Zev that didn't seem to have had much of an effect. From the turret, he scanned the faces as usual. There were so many new ones. He caught their expressions: wonder, fascination. All who could were straining for a view through the wall. Let them. The slabs would be replaced next week, or so Command had promised. Just make sure nothing happens in the meantime. Zev glanced over at the gap. So far, so good. All morning, soldiers had been moving around, shifting debris and reinforcing the wire barrier hastily put up last night. Others, their rifles pointed down, but ready, had watched the people on the other side of the wire. The soldiers' heads moved back and forth, back and forth, so many mechanical dolls searching for danger in the crowd—the focused eye, the hand moving with something in it, a sudden rush toward the opening.

Two mounds of stacked sand bags with corrugated fiberglass roofs sat behind the wire at either end of the gap—machine-gun emplacements. Zev could just see the barrel of a weapon sticking out of one of them. Five IDF troop carriers were parked just beyond the gun emplacement. More than enough firepower. The breech in the wall had been sealed. It would be back to normal soon.

* * *

Hussein, Mumtaz, and Malik were in a three-story building just over the hill, in an apartment on the top floor that afforded a decent view of the opening in the wall. Each was holding binoculars to his eyes, but stayed in the shadows, not wishing to provide a convenient target. They knew the IDF would be combing these buildings with video surveillance to see who showed up to look. A quick call and a missile could be launched from a gunship they neither saw nor heard. Not a risk they wanted to take.

The concrete slabs lay in a heap, a fine layer of dust beginning to cover them, like remnants of yet another past civilization. So many of those in this part of the world. The view suddenly struck Hussein as funny.

"The walls of Jericho, and the Promised Land behind it."

He smiled at the perversity of it.

"Blasphemy!"

Malik grimaced as if to rid himself of a bad taste and looked around for a place to spit, but they were in someone's apartment, and the rules of hospitality said he couldn't. Hussein scanned the gap beyond the razor wire. There was no motion, not a sign of life. Just the machine gun emplacements and the armored vehicles sitting silent, waiting.

Hussein moved his view to the left, where a throng of people was bunched together, staring at the ruined concrete. Multiple coils of razor wire ran at ground level in front of them, so their vision was obscured a bit, but the crowd could certainly see through the gap to the settlement on the ridge beyond, framed by the slabs that had managed to remain standing. Hussein trained his binoculars on the settlement, its high wall giving it a posture of removal from everything around it. He supposed the crusaders' fortresses had once looked a bit like this. They were mostly all in ruins now, their grandeur humbled. He focused on a group of black-clad men, their clothing stark against the light browns and greens of summer. Each wore a white, knitted *kipa* and cradled an Uzi. The men were standing in the approach road to the settlement, staring back through the opening in the wall. Hussein guessed that most of the settlers were hidden or inside, watching, waiting to see what would happen today, staying clear of any imagined line of fire.

Hussein wondered what the settlers' view was like. What did they see framed there? He lowered the binoculars. From the window he saw what was on this side of the wall: the old olive grove; a couple of stained, undistinguished apartment buildings; laundry hanging out windows; a small garden here and there. Signs of lives and routines. He raised the binoculars. The men hadn't moved. They just stared. Hussein smiled again at the thought of what had to be their disbelief.

"There they are, staring at us as if we had emerged from nowhere. And maybe we have."

Hussein turned his gaze back to the people on this side. He was sure he couldn't see all of them. The crowd filled the space between the road and the wall, right up to the rolls of razor wire. He could also see what looked like another large crowd in the distance, where the wire ended and butted against the wall itself.

Hussein lowered the binoculars and looked at the broken pile of concrete. What did the crowd see? From his vantage point, the great slabs lay like the dominos they were. With his unmagnified eye, the people were reduced to insects in a junkyard, scurrying among the refuse.

But something was there he couldn't see.

"I'm going to get closer."

Hussein put down his binoculars.

"I'll be back."

Malik nodded. Mumtaz moved to go with him.

"No, I need to go alone."

Mumtaz grunted disapproval.

"It's not safe."

"I'll be fine."

Mumtaz shrugged.

Hussein descended to the street and took a circuitous route among the buildings to come out on the low edge of the olive grove, a couple of hundred meters from the gap. He looked back. Every track through the trees was a flow of bodies. But instead of remaining on the hillside, the crowd was filling the space behind the line of throwers, the thin rivulets from the hillside pooling into a great body, deepening by the minute, threatening to overflow.

It struck Hussein that everyone was quiet; there was no singing, no chanting, only a few words of conversation here and there. Yesterday, he had heard the singing. But now, nothing. Perhaps it was too much, too incredible. Too confusing. Too powerful? Awe renders you mute. He thought he understood that much at least. He hoped so.

He needed to get nearer to the gap. To see for himself.

He joined one of the lines flowing down to the wall, matching his pace to the others who were now beside and around him. At the bottom of the hill, he found himself surrounded by hundreds of people standing shoulder to shoulder, all looking up at the wall. Hussein elbowed his way forward to near the front of the crowd. Here, everyone was silent. Hussein looked over the shoulder of the man in front of him. The multiple coils of razor wire were in the way, of course, but they couldn't begin to hide the pile of fallen concrete rising behind and the settlement outlined against the sky. The leaves of the trees in the olive grove on the other side of the wall flickered in the warm yellow light of the afternoon. The shadows were lengthening, giving dimension to the scene, filling out the forms of the landscape, giving to each object, each rock, each tree, each clump of grass, a new substance, as if they were inhaling the light, drinking it in.

Hussein looked at each fallen slab—the jagged shards that had broken off from them in the collapse, the earth that they were sinking into, the dust that was shrouding them. What was once so ominous was now waste; what was so powerful was now impotent. Then it struck him, and he understood the awe felt by the crowd. The blocks lay like toppled statues of heathen gods of antiquity, their once-implacable hold over man shattered in the dirt. The gods under whose thumb his people had been oppressed were dead at their feet. Part of him felt the lifting of his heart, pushing him to shout out loud and dance in the street. He hadn't understood this last night. He had cheered the humiliation of the Israelis, the collapse of this greatest symbol of their omnipotence, but now he felt something more, something in the hearts of the crowd. A god had died: the silent wall still stretched into the distance, but it was now mortal. The foreign god, the god of the conqueror, was dead, as dead as Baal or Osiris or Marduk, all gods who had once ruled this land and who now were dust, nothing but faded inscriptions on broken stones. Their statues lay impotent in heaps, in the ruins of ancient cities whose names had been forgotten.

He, too, had believed in this god; they all had. They had feared this god and its wrath and by doing so had worshipped it. He had let himself be sucked into a ritual of human sacrifice, trussing himself for slaughter and delivering himself willingly to the altar, time and time again, in a pitiless cycle of vengeance and retribution. The god of conquest and destruction, the god of oppression and slavery, the god of death and revenge, this god was a false god. And he realized that it was not his god, it was a pagan god, a foreign god. Not the god of the prophets at all. He felt drained by the thought of it, yet at the same time lighter, freer, as if he had run a race with a load on his back and now, having finished, had tossed the load away.

* * *

Idith was stuck at a checkpoint several kilometers away. Traffic was backed up, gridlocked as far as she could see. She noticed, though, that people were leaving their cars and walking back, away from the checkpoint, out of sight. On an impulse, she opened her door and got out. A stream of mute figures was moving around a bend in the road. When she got

268

past the curve, she saw that people were walking up and around a large hill. The route would take them several kilometers away from the direct route to Qalunya, but by now she knew enough about the local terrain to see that, unless there was an immediate deployment of enough troops to block their way, they would make it, at length, to the gap. The ritual was hours away, if it was going to take place. As she got in step with a group of women, some quite young, some older than she by the look of them, she wondered what they would find.

* * *

As the time for the ritual approached, the line began to form. Men and women stepped forward holding their bags of rocks. Zev had once thought they looked like school children carrying lunch bags. Naïve and harmless. No longer. Yet he felt no fear. He had always kept his distance from fear. Fear was for his targets. Fear interrupted objectivity, disturbed calculation, his two closest friends in the field. How many times had he been told, "Fear is your friend. It keeps you alive"? But he was not afraid. Not now.

Dani returned from below after talking with Command again.

"We have two gunships on standby, just in case. But orders are to sit back and not engage unless an attempt is made to breach the wire."

"Yes, Dani."

The two soldiers took their positions. The line of throwers stretched in each direction as far as either soldier could see. Men and women standing shoulder to shoulder, waiting. The dense crowd of watchers stood unbroken just behind. There was no sound, only a soft breeze that helped cut the heat. Dani looked at the long string of forms with stones in their hands. There were over a thousand at least, he was sure.

* * *

Idith had reached the olive grove. She was tired and sweat had glued her shirt to her back. But she felt exhilarated. The rising wind filled the cloth, lifting it, drying her off as she took her place in the line.

There was motion on the hillside, and Aisha came into view. The men escorting her held back and she walked down alone, making her way over to where the gap was. When she reached flat ground, the crowd parted to let her through. She reached the razor wire and stopped. Extending her hand, she touched a barb on the wire and a drop of blood appeared on her fingertip.

She looked across where the wall had fallen. The gap reached up to the sky. The void was filled with light. Its shell lay splintered at her feet. In the distance, the olive trees thrived in the sun. The wall had only hidden them, not erased them. She saw how the soldiers and their guns clung to the wall and its shadow, but the shadow couldn't reach her here. It was too far for that particular darkness to reach now.

The broken concrete slabs were already covered with a powdering of dust, their hard edges softened, blunted. The earth was drawing them down, back into itself, humbling their presumption. How infinite the slabs had seemed; how shallow they were to her now. And in this place, their pull was gone. She had no need to struggle, to keep her balance. She would not be pitched into nothingness. She exhaled and dropped her eyes, and then she closed them to feel release, comfort. She was weightless and warm, her body floating in the light.

But she had to open her eyes again and look up. Because she felt the pull again, weaker, but it was there, thrashing at the sides of the gap, in the shadows that the wall still cast far to her left and right. She exhaled again and let her feet feel the earth hold them steady as she turned and walked toward the place where she had first thrown a stone against the wall. The throwers and the crowd were silent as she passed in front of them. Her feet took her in measured paces, heavy but firm.

* * *

Aisha stopped at the familiar patch of ground and looked at the wall before her. She had thrown so many stones; the concrete was divotted and scarred. But it still stood. She was still for a long moment, taking several deep breaths, each slower, fuller than the last. Then she took a stone into her hand, and the ritual began yet again.

Despite the heat, Aisha maintained the even rhythm of her task, her small, dark figure leading the masses behind her —speaking a name, casting a stone, listening as hundreds of other voices repeated the name, cast their stones, waiting for the clatter to die away before she spoke the next name. From his viewpoint, as always, Zev could see the arcs of the stones curl toward the wall down the length of the line. It was like watching surf pounding the bottom of a cliff, crashing, receding, rising again—persistence against immobility.

Stones hit the razor wire, too, and it cast off flickering light, as if the fallen slabs were on fire, as if they would consume themselves. The motion of the wire grew until it was writhing in the sun. It looked in pain.

As the throwing continued, the spectators on the hillside began to feel the wind rise and were grateful for the promised relief. But even as the wind cooled them, they saw the sky begin to darken. Something had disturbed the soil, for it rose up in the air, and the wind in the distance began to take on a fluid shape, a semi-transparent mass of dust and dirt in the shade of the surrounding hills. It blew down the slope along the length of the wall, where it twisted and turned as it slammed into the tall concrete bisecting the valley. Rebuffed, the wind broke as surf on the face of the barrier, rising up and falling back on itself, its swell then rising again, pushing against the wall. The wind bore down upon the throwers, embracing them in its depths. The stones continued to arc toward the wall, and as each wave now hit, the chips that burst off were suspended in the dust. They sparkled in the angled light, and the wind took on the substance of something vital and alive.

A strong gust came and obscured most of Zev's view through the scope. He lowered it and looked out to see the whole length of wall in front of him immersed for an instant in a series of swirling masses of dust. He watched, mesmerized. Individual gusts, revelling in their new forms, climbed and twirled between the throwers and the wall. The throwers remained unhindered, however, and each wave of stones crackled on impact with the concrete, sending up more sparks to give life to the air.

Dust rose to the turret and engulfed it. Zev fell to the floor, heaving and struggling for air. The gas masks were below. There was no time. Zev choked, covered his face with his hands and curled himself up against the swirling grit. Then it settled on him, a thick powder in his nose, his mouth. He spat and gasped for air. It tasted raw, harsh. Standing, he could see soldiers lying, kneeling, coughing. The rear doors of the troop carriers were open, and the men who had been inside were sprawled on the ground, heaving, retching.

* * *

273

Aisha threw her last stone, and as the others followed suit, a dense column of wind and dust shot up into the air from all around her, and she was completely engulfed in the whirling mass. It embraced and caressed her for a few brief instants, then it expanded, until everyone around, watchers as well as throwers, was awash in a tide of soil suspended in the air. The wind rose and swirled, twisting and diving, dancing in the moment. Then it stopped and the dirt dropped away with the echoes of the impacts of the stones from up the line, leaving everyone dazed with the suffocating, exhilarating sensation of having been immersed in the very earth that now lay at their feet as before.

Aisha remained standing, her hands by her sides, facing the wall. Zev looked at her again through his scope. Aisha's head, hair, and clothes were now filthy, and she was looking straight ahead, at what he couldn't tell. He dialed the scope in to see closer. Her face filled the lens. It was caked with dirt; rivulets of sweat were cutting through it, moving down her cheeks. But the contours they followed were new to him. It was the same face, but it was a different face. The girl was gone. The witch was gone. A woman remained.

Her expression was odd, though. He couldn't tell what it was, certainly nothing like exuberance or triumph or joy. No, she was just standing there, looking at the wall. He couldn't put his finger on it, but the way she stood, her whole being looked, well, swelling, with a potent, surging calm. The calm of the ocean, pounding against the shore, over and over, easily, without hurry, but implacable, inevitable. He swung his scope around to try to discover what she was looking at, but all he could see was the pockmarked face of the concrete. It looked eroded and old. Mortal. He shrugged and swung his scope back, but she had turned and was walking away, back up the hill toward the olive grove.

About the Author

Timothy Niedermann is a graduate of Kenyon College and attended the Albert-Ludwigs Universität in Freiburg-im-Breisgau, Germany. He also holds a J.D. from Case Western Reserve University Law School. *Wall of Dust* is his first novel.

ACKNOWLEDGMENTS

Many people have contributed to this book, in many different ways. I would like to thank my initial readers, who gave encouraging feedback on the early drafts of *Wall of Dust* and confirmed that what I had written had value. To Ghada Arafat, the very first person to comment and who gave critical suggestions that improved the credibility of this book enormously, my heartfelt thanks. To my other early readers, who confirmed so much and gave me confidence in what I had written: Luset Kohen Fins, Reema Batheeb, Imen Benyoub, Ellin Rosenthal, Catherine Lockwood, Piper McDermott, Doug Elerath, Gary Deckard, and Anthony Charles Bash. I am in your debt. And to Nada Sneige Fuleihan, whose encouragement has pushed me to make this book the best it can be, I am forever grateful.

Next, to my publisher, Ian Shaw, who, having lived in Gaza and travelled extensively in the West Bank, was able to suggest small but important changes that have given additional depth to the story, my unbound gratitude. I am lucky to have found Deux Voiliers Publishing. Thanks to Caroline Vu, my fellow author at DVP, for her astute comments, and to DVP's insightful copy editor and meticulous proofreader Liz McKeen.

Last, to my family, close and extended, who have waited so long for this book to appear—my parents and siblings, of course, and especially to my patient wife Sue and my wonderful children, to whom *Wall of Dust* is dedicated—to all of you, my love and gratitude for your extraordinary patience and support.

About Deux Voiliers Publishing

Organized as a writers-plus collective, Deux Voiliers Publishing is a new generation publisher. We focus on emerging Canadian writers. The art of creating new works of fiction is our driving force.

We are proud to have published *Wall of Dust* by Timothy Niedermann.

Other Works of Fiction published by Deux Voiliers Publishing

Soldier, Lily, Peace and Pearls by Con Cú (Literary Fiction 2012)

Kirk's Landing by Mike Young (Crime/Adventure 2014)

Sumer Lovin' by Nicole Chardenet (Humour/Fantasy 2013)

Last of the Ninth by Stephen Lorne Bennett (Historical Fiction 2012)

Marching to Byzantium by Brendan Ray (Historical Fiction 2012)

Tales of Other Worlds by Chris Turner (Fantasy/Sci-Fiction 2012)

Romulus by Fernand Hibbert and translated by Matthew Robertshaw (Historical Fiction/English Translation 2014)

Bidong by Paul Duong (Literary Fiction 2012)

Zaidie and Ferdele by Carol Katz (Illustrated Children's Fiction 2012)

Palawan Story by Caroline Vu (Literary Fiction 2014)

Cycling to Asylum by Su J. Sokol (Speculative Fiction 2014)

Stage Business by Gerry Fostaty (Crime 2014)

Stark Nakid by Sean McGinnis (Crime/Humour 2014)

Twisted Reasons by Geza Tatrallyay (International Crime Thriller 2014)

Four Stones by Norman Hall (Canadian Spy Thriller 2015)

Nothing to Hide by Nick Simon (Dystopian Fiction 2015)

Frack Off by Jason Lawson (Humour/Political Satire 2015)

Please visit our website for ordering information
www.deuxvoilierspublishing.com

www.ingramcontent.com/pod-product-compliance
Lightning Source LLC
Chambersburg PA
CBHW022028240626
47154CB00007B/2312